I0659128

Life Ain't Been No
Crystal Stair

L. Hicks

Extreme Overflow Publishing
Dacula, GA
USA

Extreme Overflow
PUBLISHING
Dacula, GA
USA

Extreme Overflow Publishing
A Brand of Extreme Overflow Enterprises, Inc
P.O. Box 1811
Dacula, GA 30019

www.extremeoverflow.com
Send feedback to info@extreme-overflow-enterprises.com

Printed in the United States of America

Editing by Extreme Overflow Publishing Editors
Cover Design by Extreme Overflow Publishing

Library of Congress Catalogin-Publication
Data is available for this title. ISBN: 978-0-9989351-8-8

Table of Content

Preface .... Pg 4

Chapter One FOUNDATION .... Pg 7

Chapter Two DISCONTENT .... Pg 15

Chapter Three THE CORNERSTONE .... Pg 22

Chapter Four HIS SENIOR LOOKING FOR A Pg 30
JUNIOR ....

Chapter Five FLEEKS IN THE CRYSTAL ..... Pg 42

Chapter Six LILY .... Pg 67

Chapter Seven BUTTERMILK .... Pg 79

Chapter Eight A LIGHT IN THE CRYSTAL .... Pg 100

Chapter Nine DIRTY GLASS .... Pg 111

Chapter Ten TRANSLUCENT .... Pg 127

Chapter Eleven BROKEN GLASS .... Pg 138

Chapter Twelve STAIRWAY TO HEAVEN .... Pg 150

Chapter Thirteen CHARCOAL .... Pg 157

Chapter Fourteen THE CRYSTAL STAIR .... Pg 167

Afterword .... Pg 173

Preface

I never expected I'd be in this is situation.

There I was, living life the way I thought it should be lived. Doing what I could to make ends meet and provide for my son. Showing him how to push past obstacles, despite the circumstances. Then I got hit with a bomb.

Stage Three Colon Cancer.

Devastated is a word that doesn't remotely describe how I felt. My health began to decline rapidly. I was terrified. Terrified that I wouldn't be afforded the chance to watch my son grow up. Terrified that my life was soon to end earlier than it began. Terrified that I'd leave this earth knowing I'd found love in all the wrong places and not be able to experience it the way I knew I could. The way I knew I should.

Then my grandmother came.

Mom petitioned for my grandmother, then in her early seventies, to come stay with me. Help care for me while she worked. There was much to handle. Caring for a cancer-stricken daughter and her seven-year-old son, while working a full-time job, seemed nearly impossible. Ends needed to be met. What I didn't know is when my grandmother came to help care for me, that I'd learn her story.

My grandmother never talked much about her past. I knew bits and pieces but not to the extent that my grandmother shared. Surviving an abusive husband, raising eighteen children, with only twelve of them being her own, and having to restart life as she knew it.

The main take away from that conversation is, when life looks bleak, all you have to do is add a little Windex to the glass, so that you can see more clear. In the months to come, my grandmother shared her story, which in turn, inspired this book.

Within these pages, I hope the story of *Roxie Rae Farrow* inspires you just as it did me.

I hope that wherever you are in your journey, that it speaks to you in some way and pushes you to keep going. That whatever demons you *think* you have, it's all just an illusion. That what you experience, is only there to make you stronger and more invincible. Life isn't always going to be easy. Challenges are part of the ebb and flow. Just know, whatever your belief, that higher power will never steer you wrong.

Chapter One

Foundation

I ain't never heard no sound like that before. It was this loud boom that rang in my ear. Almost like one of those firecrackers they let loose during Fourth of July, but louder. Not like I ain't know he kept the shotguns, yes more than one, up on the wall over the bed. He was crazier than a bed bug and I married his behind.

He knew I wouldn't fight back.

The light cries from my babies taunted me. That eerie silence with their young voices in the background, sent a nasty chill up my arms. I wanted to run 'cross the hall and tell 'em I was OK. That we were OK, but he had the door blocked, so I couldn't run and check on 'em.

They were just as scared as I was.

He stood there mockin' me. Talkin' somethin' slick that I ain't even pay 'tention to. That old, sweaty musk on his body. I thought I'd be used to it by now, but that never happened. I could almost tell the type of women he was wit that night and it was more than one. The aura of whatever brown liquor he chose to lose hisself in that night, came through right along with that same musky scent.

Had the gun pointed in my direction as if he was gon kill me. It was the first time I feared for me and not because of dyin'. I could careless at that point. It was more me being afraid 'bout who the heck was gon take care of my babies. I mean, if he killed me that night, he'd just make up some lie, find another gullible woman and repeat the cycle all over again.

I couldn't have my babies in no repeat cycle.

I had to leave, but he knew I just wasn't built like that. Shoot, even I knew I wasn't built like that. No matter how bold and wild he got with his crazy, we both knew I wouldn't leave. I ain't have the heart. I wasn't a woman to take risks in that way. At least that's what I believed. What I learned some years after that night is, only you know when you've had enough. Can't nobody tell you that for sure. Everybody has a breakin' point. For as long as I could think, I ain't never thought I did, but I was wrong about myself. We were both wrong, and for my sake, I'm glad I was.

I lived in a town called Camp Hill, Alabama.

A small town wouldn't nobody think 'bout lookin' for it on a map. It wasn't all fancy like Mobile, Birmingham or Montgomery. Nothin' real famous comin' outta these here parts, despite it being almost smack dab in the middle of all three.

It's a place I often do my best to forget.

We all have some parts of our past that ain't so beautiful, and unfortunately, Camp Hill is one of those parts.

I always hear of folks talkin' 'bout their past and bein' grateful of where they came from, but Camp Hill wasn't that place for me. It's a constant reminder of all the mess I went through for simply wantin' somethin' that most people have so easy, a family.

That desire to want a family led me to make some choices that I'm not so proud of. It also showed me that I'm a lot stronger than myself, my family and my husband thought I'd be. When I do speak of that time in Camp Hill, I do my best not to sound like I'm complainin'. My life is a testimony to the things I survived. So I speak on it in a way that others can feel encouraged. It's so important to feel encouraged by someone's story. What I hope is that you find some encouragement, as well as some inspiration through my trials and triumph, because in the end, I was definitely triumphant.

My mama named me Roxie Rae Farrow a name that I loved very much. My grand papa would often tell me stories about where our last name of farrow came from. He told me that his great grandpa Farrow Gross was a slave and belonged to the Gross Plantation. Farrow had 24 chil'ren and instead of giving his kids the last name Gross he chose to give his children his first name as their last name. My grand papa said it was because he didn't want his kids to have a slave last name. He was always proud to be a Farrow and raised all his kids to be the same.

I was born a couple years before the Great

Depression and raised by my Grandpa cause my mama died when I was two. Even back then some daddies were deadbeats and mine was no different. I'd like to tell you I got some memory of my mama to hold onto like most folk, but I ain't got no recollection of her. Never even seen a picture. You can't imagine what that do to a child. I think that's one of the reasons I love my name so much because it's the only thing I have that she gave me. Well, that and a blanket that she made for me as a baby.

Funny thing 'bout my daddy is that he ain't wanna be one, but he sure knew how to waltz hisself 'round and make sure I knew it was him. But I ain't really care to know. Sometimes I wish I just said to 'em, if you ain't gon stay, don't come 'round, but I ain't have no courage to be bold like that. I know what you thinkin'. Some of ya'll feisty young peoples woulda said it, but that just ain't who I was then.

My Grandpa, Jay Farrow, was my heartbeat. He ain't never fuss or whip me. An average height man with deep brown skin, clean cut, medium build and these ol' loose curls at the top. Always stayed clean shaven around the sides when he had the chance. Wore suspenders with his slacks, and a lightweight sports coat when it wasn't too hot. Didn't shy too much away from brown, it was his color of choice.

That man sold the hell outta some good ol' moonshine.

He was the "go to" before it got 'em locked up for 'bout two years. Lucky for me, they let him out right before I was born, but his time as Grandpa ain't last too long once mama passed. In a matter of hours, he went from grandpa to daddy.

That man was sweet to me. I was his baby and he'd do anythin' to makes sure I was cared for. I now know he was the only man that ever truly loved me. Growin' up, it's how I believed a man was supposed to treat the people he loved. It's how I believed a man was 'posed to treat a woman. That's what I saw 'round my neck of the woods, protect and provide. Even as a young girl, I knew that's what I wanted. So when I ain't get it later on during my marriage, it messed me up. Made me think what I believed was fantasy, cause what I saw from the people, the families that lived 'round me, wasn't even close to what went on behind closed doors.

I discovered that first hand.

Only spent about twelve years of my life in that tiny house I grew up in on the end of Route

25. Sometimes, Grandpa would pull out a couple of coins he kept stashed from his moonshine days, and we'd head into town. Those days, I'd stop inside Mr. Tucker's Drugstore and grab as much penny candy as I could fill a paper bag wit. It ain't happen often. Made sure I got plenty pieces of chewing gum, candy suckers and peppermints. I liked those the best.

Even though Grandpa worked, we was poor.

He did three days a week on a sharecropper's farm with our neighbor Mr. Johnson. The farm was 'bout half mile down the road. Those fourteen hour shifts helped him make enough money to get us an icebox and a good furnace for us to cook and make stew. Even made a fireplace where he'd chop wood to keep us warm during the evenings. For years, I thought that makeshift mattress wit straw, some chicken feathers and whatever my cousin Sara could conjure up, was the best resting place I had. I'd wrap myself up in the old blankets my mama made when she was alive. Seemed like it was the only connection I had to her. Our house was old and raggedy. Plenty of nights, we would see snakes and critters coming through the holes in the house. I would just close my eyes and pray they ain't bite me.

This life was the only thing I knew. Even

though my lil heart and mind felt there was somethin' bigger out there, I ain't know how to get it. Figured I'd get some schoolin' under me, work good, marry me an even better man and make my way outta Camp Hill.

I always wanted to make my way outta Camp Hill.

It wasn't like I ain't think there was nothin' for me here. I just knew there was so much more outside this small town. More that would give me an opportunity to have the things I always wanted. I had aunts in Birmingham, so I always thought I'd end up there. What I'd come to find out is, what I believed was opportunity and freedom, shifted in ways I never thought possible. And trust me, it wasn't like what they taught you in school.

Chapter Two

Discontent

I hated being poor. At ten, I made the decision that I wasn't gonna live poor and have a good life by any means necessary. Just ain't realize how long it was gon take me to achieve it.

Back then, Birmingham was the place where a new life was possible. We called it the "Big City." Before she moved out there, Cousin Sara stayed with Grandpa and me for a few years. Folks always say they had good jobs and even better lookin' men, but I ain't never find out.

All us kids was poor at school, some might have had a little bit more than others, but we all didn't really have much.

After while you get tired of wearin' old hand-me-downs from cousins and takin' old worn out strips of leather to patch up the holes in your shoes. Ain't like the repairs last long. When you gotta walk eight miles to and from school every day in the heat on a rocky, dirt road, ain't much patchin' up one can do. So I gave up, and just learned how to make due and ignore the stares from some of the other kids.

Ya'll young people think ya'll had stress at ya'lls age? Wonder how you'd fair during my day. No matter what time you grew up in, worrin' at that age 'bout how you look, who liked you and all the other stuff you find out later, don't really matter. Is no way for chil'ren to be livin'. At such a young age, you teach yaself that, what people think about you matters, and that ya own happiness depends on those peoples you tryna please.

That was the biggest lesson I had to unlearn.

I just couldn't find no happiness in much of anything. I knew Grandpa loved me, but I wanted to have both my parents just like the other kids. It always looked like it was a better life to live, but it just wasn't in the cards for me. You realize later, those experiences growin' up shape how you make decisions as an adult.

Be mindful of that.

I ain't know how to cope with how I felt.

Peoples ain't go to therapists and stuff like they do now, so I kept all that quiet and to myself. I'd always be doodlin' in school. Drawin' circles and lines, thinkin' I'd be able to find a way to connect the dots somehow. The sad part is that, those thoughts ain't go pass that piece of paper. Teachers always used to say my head was in the clouds. I ain't know what that meant, but it sho nuff seem like the clouds had it better than me.

Walkin' to and from school pretty much was the time I'd used to think about my life now, and the life I really wanted for myself. I walked the trail alone, moved at my own pace, looked around at the sky and trees, tried to find somethin' different each day. Some days, my eyes and I were on the same page. Some days we weren't.

I always imagine mama was walkin' wit me. I'm certain she watched over me during those long lonely walks.

Along the trail, I'd search for some edible mushrooms. Those small potatoes that grew from the ground, along with some roots and other herbs, then place 'em in a burlap sack I'd borrow from Grandpa. There were river birch trees on the trail, but there was one off to the side that no one paid 'tention to, I'd hide what I'd find there and pick it up on the way home. With the scraps I found, Grandpa was able to make good stew. Always felt like I made things just a bit easier for him when I had something to bring home.

One mornin', I was runnin' a bit behind in gettin' ready for school. On a good day, the walk was an hour and half and I woke up about fifteen minutes after the rooster crowed. I was lucky Grandpa ain't have a shift that day. He helped me get dressed and out the door.

I ran as fast as I could.

Had to stop and catch my breath a few times. The hole on the patched up shoes I'd been savin' was startin' to rip. Felt the tears tryin' to come out, but I held it in as long as I could. 'Bout midway down the trail, I was stopped dead in my tracks by a mule. It must've had rabies or sumthin' cause it was foamin' at the mouth and grindin' its hoof 'gainst the dirt ready to charge at me.

Life Ain't Been No Crystal Stair

The sweat gushed down my face.

It was so hot that day I could smell the musk from me and the mule swirlin' in the air. The silence 'tween us both was deafenin'. My heart beat 'gainst my chest so hard, it felt like my rib cage was 'bout to crack. The beast gave out a loud cry and charged at me. I was a statue, lettin' the pee drip down my leg in fear. Before it could knock me down, Grandpa ran behind it and hit it over the head with a tree trunk. He beat that thang somethin' awful. When he was done, I screamed and he grab me in his arms.

I was OK with missin' school that day.

Grandpa gave me a hot bath, heated up some milk he got from the farm, and let me sleep.

Found another trail to take after that day.

From that point on, Grandpa would walk me halfway and I'd walk the rest. I enjoyed our mornin' time together. He'd tell me about all the crazy people he worked with on the farm and how to deal with the white folk. It was a routine I'd become use to, so when it changed, that shift was hard to adjust.

One mornin', I got up and got myself ready to do my usual walk with Grandpa to school. It was unusually cool that day, so I went in the closet to grab my sweater and realized he wasn't up yet. I went in his room, called him several times with no answer. I got scared. Grandpa slept hard but not to where he wouldn't hear me. I called his name again and again. I knew the second I called and he ain't answer, he was gone. Just couldn't imagine God took him away from me.

Didn't make sense.

Ain't know nobody same age as me, that ain't at least have they grandparents. Turns out, knowing myself was enough.

I was heartbroken.

He was all I knew.

It was like I was two all over again with no one and no family. My mama, daddy and now Grandpa, gone.

Back then, they'd have the body stay in the house for couple weeks before the funeral and burial. He was in the front near the fireplace he built, so I'd sit there and talk to him as if he could hear me. I cried every day. If this was what a broken heart felt like, I ain't need to date no man to feel it. Once Grandpa was in the ground, I was made to live with Uncle Willie and Aunt Martha, my mama's brother and his wife. I tried to be excited about it. Always thought about havin' a different life, but I never thought Grandpa wouldn't be 'round to see it.

A couple days later, I moved in with Uncle Willie on the opposite side of town. His house was much bigger. Even had my own room. As sad as I was, the thought of having clothes that weren't worn or hand-me-down, made the move a little easier.

Chapter Three

The Cornerstone

C an you imagine cooking for a family of seven? I couldn't but I did it. When I moved in with Uncle Willie and Aunt Martha, I was twelve. The school year was 'bout to end, so I picked up a job working on the plantation, chopping cotton with Mr. Billmore. I had a three-day schedule like Grandpa and would switch times from early mornin' before school and after school. He paid me $.03 per pound and that was a lot back then for somebody like me. Anything would do me good. Figured maybe he felt bad cause I ain't have no parents. He was one of the few white people, back then, that was nice to me.

Life Ain't Been No Crystal Stair

On days I ain't work at Mr. Billmore's, I'd cook dinner. It was hard the first few times, but I caught on. Aunt Martha was there to guide me along the way. One night she made chicken with brown gravy. I ain't ever had meat so soft and buttery.

It was seasoned so well.

I ain't know much about Aunt Martha but she sure knew how to cook, and I made sure she taught me how to make that chicken. It's one of the many things I learned from her that I made really well.

Workin' was good for me 'cause I was able to buy better clothes and shoes. The next year, I finished elementary school, and that fall went to junior high. Lawd knows, I was glad I ain't have to walk through those woods no more. We lived close enough for me to even do a quick wash up after workin' in the fields.

Bein' around other chil'ren made me not feel so lonely anymore. I'd meet more people and talk more. Livin' with grandpa, I was always alone. There was days I use to cry, wishin' I had someone to play with. Now I had friends, which helped me work my way outta bein' so daggone shy. The job with Mr. Billmore helped me with that too.

First couple of days of school, I met Delilah

and Bunnie Mae. At the time, they were the only ones who spoke to me in class. Delilah was the pretty one. Always wore her hair in a bun. Her dress had these fancy lace patterns. She had this rose-colored, sandy brown skin and green eyes, with a small hint of light brown, that looked like caramel in the middle. Even had pretty teeth. The boys and the men flirted with her all the time. To be honest, the boys flirted with all the light-skinned girls. Me, I'd be lucky if I got a boy to smile back, let alone talk to me.

Me and Bunnie Mae were 'bout the same color, but I was just a touch darker. She was a warm, chestnut brown and I was more copper. And whew lawd, did Bunnie Mae have a shape! Honey, she had a curve 'round dem hips and a large behind. I ain't never seen nobody our age shaped like that. Dem lil nasty boys would try to slide they hands up her dress and she'd smack 'em.

Bunnie was feisty, nothing like her name.

Her and I both wore pigtails. Hers were a bit longer than mine and she'd have these ribbons in her hair that match her dress. Always wore blue and white, ain't never seen that girl in no other color.

Aunt Martha showed me how to sew my own

clothes since she was a seamstress in town. She'd bring home those same lace patterns and let me have it. I ain't wanna seem like I was copyin' Delilah, so I'd put 'em in places people wouldn't expect — along the bust line and the zipper, even sewed some around the sleeves and down the inseam of the dress. Tried to make myself stand out enough to get a hello.

Some days it worked, some days it didn't.

The girls never judged me.

We'd have lunch at school and walk home together afterward. I was happy to have other girls that I could talk to. We would giggle all day everyday and it felt good to laugh. I rarely ever laughed livin with my grand papa. And chile, Bunnie's mouth was fresh! The way that gurl cuss, wouldn't nobody know how smart she is.

Sometimes, I wish I was outspoken like Bunnie Mae. Even Delilah had a bit of sass, but I ain't ever had the courage to speak like they did. I was taught, it's better for girls to be seen and not heard, so I just went along to get along. Wasn't in me to sass nobody. Even when it came time to defend myself, I just kept my feelins' inside.

There was one boy in school who'd catch

my eye.

He was sorta cute. Could tell he was smart by those black frames he wore. Seemed like all the smart boys were those type of glasses. We'd wave at each other passin' through the halls. Both of us were so shy, that's far as we got.

In my teenage years, I had this need to feel grounded in somethin', like I needed roots or a stronghold. I was happy to have other girls that I could talk to. We would giggle all day everyday and it felt good to laugh. I rarely ever laughed livin with grandpa. I'd see plenty people headin' to church down the road. Never heard Grandpa talkin' bout God unless he cussed or was in pain. Other than that, I ain't know much about 'em.

I was up early one Sunday and heard the church bell ring. Decided to see what went on inside. I put on a black top and a pink skirt I got from the store in town, and headed to the service. Uncle Willie ain't make a big issue 'bout me 'tending church. It was my choice whether I went or not. Down the street was Fairmount Baptist Church, where Rev. C.B. Ludlow was the Pastor. I ain't know what to expect when I walked in that Sunday, but I knew somethin' good was 'bout to happen.

Life Ain't Been No Crystal Stair

I'll never forget his sermon.

Just so happen that day, Pastor spoke 'bout loneliness and it felt as if I were in the right place at the right time. He told us to pick up the Bible and read the 73rd Psalm. I never read a Bible before, so I did my best to follow along. Three verses, twenty-three through twenty-six, struck a chord wit me. Spoke to me so much, that I took time to memorize 'em. When I felt alone, I'd recite 'em to myself:

Yet I am always with you; you hold me by my right hand.

You guide me with your counsel, and afterward you will take me into glory.

Whom have I in heaven but you? And Earth has nothing I desire besides you.

My flesh and my heart may fail, but God is the strength of my heart and my portion forever.

I felt the strength of the Lord in those verses.

As if He were next to me as I read 'em.

Pastor reminded us that, even when people forsake us, when our friends abandon us, when our family members pass on, the Lord will always be there.

Through good and bad times, He is our stronghold. The bedrock of our faith, the Cornerstone. He's the force, the glue that keeps us togetha when the world turns cruel and wants to break us down.

He said, God is the light in our darkest hour, as well as the peace in our hearts. His love fills us and gives us glory, and because of that, the Lord is somethin' to rejoice about. Because, no matter our shortcomings, or how dusty and dirty we believe our souls to be, God will always choose us. He'll never turn us away. We're nothin more than a spiritual bath away from righteousness. That alone, sold me on the gift of God in my life.

I joined the church the same day, and the next Sunday, I was baptized. It was the first time in my life I felt happy. Years later, I'd have to hang onto that feelin', 'cause it was the only thing I had left.

Being in the church helped me with school since there were other chil'ren my age there. My cousins weren't going as regular as I was, but I knew in order to make somethin' of myself, I needed all the education I could get. So, I continued on and finished. I graduated from the ninth to the tenth grade and the school gave us a small ceremony. Uncle Willie and Aunt Martha was proud of me but they ain't come.

Life Ain't Been No Crystal Stair

Those are the times I wish I had a mama.

Not havin' family 'round to be part of in my biggest moment in my life made me feel sad. That same lonely feeling showed up when it was time to get my certificate. In that moment, I remembered the verses from 73rd Psalm and recited them as I waited to receive my award. I walked up to the principal, and the sun shined through the windows of the school house. It was a reminder that I wasn't alone, and that God was with me. I could almost feel Him huggin' me. His reward for me stayin' strong and trustin' in Him. It further confirmed my faith in the Lord.

In hindsight, maybe it wasn't meant for none of my family to be there. Can't say whether or not the same feelin' would've occurred, but maybe I would've given my family too much of the faith I needed to invest in God. Some of that recognition is what would soon hold me together.

Chapter Four

His Senior
Looking For A Junior

It was 1945, almost near the end of World War II. Until I figured out my next move, I continued workin' on Mr. Billmore's plantation. I was savin' up money, but I hadn't decided for what just yet. I became more visible in the church. Joined different ministries and helped out where I could. Discovered I was good at plannin' events, so I did a lot of outreach in the neighborhood.

One evenin', I teamed up with Lula Blackwell.

Her and I were to help raise money for the church. She had a fish fry' at her house, which I thought was gonna be small but turned out to be larger than both us thought. People were there from all over town. I did what I could as host and kept track of whatever people donated.

A few hours into the night, I came 'cross this good lookin' man who I noticed had been starin' at me most of the night, hard. We'd catch eyes a couple times, but I thought nothin' of it. All the women there were droolin' over him, and he ate it all up.

It was the peak of summer in Camp Hill, which meant nothing but heat.

The mysterious man had on a white tank, army pants and some black combat boots. He made sure everyone knew he was military and just got back in the States from Germany. Bragged about servin' with a few Tuskegee Airmen and had plenty of stories to share.

He kept the women, and some of the men, entertained.

Boy was he a talker.

Tried to talk with me a few times, but I was too shy and brushed him off. Followed me around a lil throughout the night. Lula must've noticed, cause every time he'd come 'round, she'd grab my arm and drag me to another part of the house. Women would be talkin' to 'em and he'd stop the conversation and walk over to me. Made me feel a bit uncomfortable. I ain't want no trouble with any of these women. I did what I could helping Lula out and kept track of the money that people gave us.

After while, he stopped, but he'd stare to catch my eye when the chance came 'round. Figured my shyness put 'em off, but he stayed 'round a bit longer after the party, while Lula and I cleaned up. Her attitude changed and I couldn't figure out why. She rushed me off and decided to finish cleanin' up herself. It was late, so I ain't really mind it. The man waved bye to me as I left. I was hopin' he ain't ask to walk me home, cause it would be hard for me to say no. Camp Hill ain't had no street lights like they do now, so anything coulda happen 'tween Lula and Uncle Willie's house.

But he stood there.

Thought that was the last I seen him, until he showed up next day at Uncle Willie's. Asked me to go and get a bite to eat. He must've followed me home anyway and found out where I lived.

Life Ain't Been No Crystal Stair

I was nervous.

Was the first time I'd ever been out with a man, or anyone for that matter. I'd soon discover, he wasn't 'round just for the moment; he was preparin' to be 'round for life.

❖ ❖ ❖

Charlie Blackwell.

Lula's brother and fourteen years my senior.

I was sixteen when we met.

Everyone called him Black because that man's skin was black as tar, but it was so smooth. Ain't seen no man since my Grandpa with skin that smooth. He was definitely a good looking fella. Back then, women loved a man who looked a lil somethin' more than just plain ol' black.

As if plain ol' black wasn't enough.

He even had this wavy hair that look like he'd put that lye in it, but I ain't never see him walkin' 'round with no chemical. Folks used to say his family was mixed with Indian, but no one knew for sure.

He was good lookin'.

He came around on days when I was working with Mr. Billmore. Uncle Willie ain't like him much 'cause he was older. Hell, he coulda been my daddy. Neither were that far apart in age.

He and I went out a couple times and I found out he had a wife and kids. Six to be exact. Us together left a lot to be talked about 'round town. His wife was nowhere to be found. I'd ask what happened, but he'd always change the subject. Didn't like talkin' bout her much. I soon got up the nerve to ask Lula. She wasn't as forthcomin' with information, but she gave me a brief run down.

The story is...

The wife spent all his money runnin' numbers in the Big City and drinkin. How she found time to travel back and forth, and raise them kids, I'll never know. Black would send money while overseas, to take care of his family, but she only used a couple dollars towards the kids, then gamble and drink up the rest. When he came home, she just up and left him and the kids. He quickly found out that that she spent every last dime. Not to mention, the rumor was that she was pregnant while he was out servin'. That nest egg Black was trying build ain't exist and it put him in a bind. The plan to live a better life and retire, became a far-fetched dream. Instead, he had to work like a dog to care for himself and the kids. After givin' his all in the service, he ended up with nothing.

Looking back, wonder if that's what stirred up the anger in his heart.

He used those buildin' skills he gained from the service, to become a lumberjack workin' at the local sawmill. Not too many people in town had a car, but he had one. A nice one. A shiny, black, 1940 Plymouth Roadking. It was fancy. Kept that thang clean like it was his child. He'd take me for rides to visit friends and family. Ain't see him much durin' the week, but we'd spend most our time on weekends.

Aunt Martha was cautious about him 'cause she thought he was lookin' for a mama for dem kids. She kept her eye on 'em just as much as Uncle Willie did. She'd always say, "Roxie be careful with him, 'cause somethin' just ain't right."

I kept that advice too far in the back of my mind.

Black was sweet to me and I liked that he was sweet to me.

'Bout a month into our relationship, he introduced me to the kids. At the time, I was only ten years ahead of his eldest, Lily. He had two more girls, Sarah and Pinky, and three boys, Dennis, Elijah and Charlie, Jr. They were quiet kids. At least that's how it seemed, and always looked a bit scruffy. Couldn't understand why, 'cause he made decent money.

Black's oldest sister Brenda took care of the kids while he was at work or out with me. Somedays, I'd walk by the house and see Lily and Pinky outside on the porch. I could feel Lily's eyes piercin' through me. Made me feel a bit uncomfortable he spent so much time with me and not those kids.

Like he was runnin' from somethin'.

We got closer within the year we met. Even made an effort to attend church wit me, but that was short-lived. Black wasn't the church going type. I'm sure he believed in God. Just never saw the purpose of church and fellowship.

With the exception of Lula, me datin' Black ain't mess up none of the friendships I had with his other sisters. Matter of fact, Brenda used to be married to my Uncle Willie. The rumor is when mama got sick, she told Brenda to raise me, but when she died, Grandpa ain't wanna let me go.

Can you imagine that? Had things been different, Black woulda been my uncle. God has a way of makin' sure yo life follow the plans He's made out for you. There's so many things I think of often and that's one of them. I'm sure my life would've turned out different had she raised me. I'da been Lily's big cousin, instead of some woman who's datin' her daddy. It's a reminder that God always has a plan.

There were even a folks in town whisperin' about Black and me. Wondered if they thought we was shackin'.

Believe me, he tried.

I was strong to my values.

He knew there was no sex before marriage, and that booger waited. It was no doubt in my mind that he probably got it from somewheres else. In fact, I'm sure of it.

But he and I stayed strong.

Ain't never had no man take a likin' to me in that way, so I knew somethin' special had to be there.

Or maybe I convinced myself it was.

Black put in a good amount of time at the sawmill and soon got promoted to supervisor. His pay increased and with the increase, came a little more pressure to get married. We talked about it many times, but I'd never give him a straight answer. As much as I wanted a family, I still felt there was somethin' more to this world than Camp Hill and wondered, would marryin' him stop me from findin' it?

We were all getting older in the house and I needed to make a decision. Uncle Willie and Aunt Martha wanted me to move to the Big City. I made the mistake of tellin' Black and he practically begged me not to leave. The conflict between wantin' to explore the world and havin' my love with Black kept me up at night. I read the Bible back to front and still couldn't find the right scripture to settle my heart. I'd grown to love him, and because he was good to me, I felt like I had to at least return the favor with marriage.

After Black and I met in the Fall of 1945, his niece wanted Brenda to move with her to Ohio. Honey, she ain't give it too much thought 'cause she left within a few weeks. That void left him with no one to help 'round the house. A few days later, he proposed but I ain't answer right away. I questioned whether being a mother to six kids was somethin' I could handle. I watched the kids at church during Sunday school, but that was only for a few hours. This required me to be an instant mama. I scared him when I didn't reply back, but three days later, I said yes to him.

Uncle Willie and Aunt Martha weren't happy with my decision.

It caused a rift with the family and became yet another important time in my life where they weren't present.

Two weeks before Thanksgiving, Black and I got married down at the courthouse. I wore this nice dress I kept saved for a special occasion. Despite Black being in the courthouse with me, I still felt alone. I whispered the verses from the 73rd Psalm during the proceedin', and hoped the Lord came down to hug on me just like he did at the graduation,but He wasn't there.

That scared me.

It scared me that the same reaction ain't happen. My stomach turned. I wanted to stop and rethink my decision, but my lips ain't move fast enough. Before I could change my mind, he and I were married.

Hindsight is truly twenty-twenty.

The next day, I moved into the house. It was the second time I moved but not the last. In a matter of days, I went from livin' in a three-bedroom house with my own room, to a two-bedroom shack. My heart sank. It wasn't like I ain't see the mess each time I walked pass. Just was naive to think looks were deceivin'. That mess outside was worse inside, and I couldn't understand why he was livin' like that 'cause he made good money.

Girls and boys ain't even had separate rooms.

Ain't make no sense how six kids slept in one bed, 'specially when the girls were developin'. Of course Black's room was the biggest, but it look like he ain't ever sleep there. Black made enough money to fix that house up and add more rooms, but he chose to live poor in a house where the roof had holes. Anybody could see the outside through the cracks in the walls.

I walked 'round that house, suitcases in hand, completely beside myself. The kids stared at me.

Couldn't tell if they were hopin' I'd run like hell or save them from this misery. To be honest, I wanted to do both. I was just too afraid to walk away. At the time, I wasn't too much worried 'bout how Black would take it. I ain't want to abandon them kids. Not like how they mama did. And back then, we ain't know nuthin' 'bout divorce and all that fancy stuff white folks could afford. I was strong in my faith and believed for better, for worse. What I ain't realize is that, things were 'bout to get worse before they could be better.

That night, Black and I did what married folks do.

Ain't never had sex before and it wasn't what I expected. All that grindin' and growlin' he did made it worse. Just wanted him to finish and get off me so I could sleep. Unfortunately, he was up on me all night, just humpin'. I fell asleep and woke up with him still humpin'. I know the Lord said be fruitful and multiply, but He could've at least made it all a bit more interestin'?

Chapter Five

Flecks in the Crystal

Took me 'bout a week to adjust and get comfortable in the kitchen. Although I knew how to make a few things, I ain't never really cook like that before. Much as I watched Grandpa and Aunt Martha make stew and other dishes, doin' it myself felt different.

Taking turns cookin' back at Uncle Willie's helped, but I had Aunt Martha to guide me through. This time I was alone and it was a hard crowd to sell. It also ain't help, we hardly had food in the house. I wanted to make oxtails, thinkin' the kids would like it and because I found it easy for me to make.

Life Ain't Been No Crystal Stair

But Black said that type of meat was too expensive. Sometimes he'd bring home a cornish hen. When I say sometimes, I mean hardly. When I say hardly, I mean once every six months, which meant twice a year. Three if we was lucky.

And that was when he was in a good mood.

Still, everyone seemed to be content with what I made. Quite honestly, it's probably 'cause they wasn't eatin' much.

I believed marriage was supposed to be a happy time.

I'd gotten the family I always wanted and a man that would take care of me. Thought it was my fairy tale come true. A lil over a month passed and my fairy tale slowly became a nightmare I couldn't wake up from. I 'spected life to be different once I got married. When I think about it, there was a difference, just not the difference I thought it'd be.

Black would be 'round durin' the work week, but when that weekend came him, his brothers and some friends I'd seen 'round town, would go to the local bar and get just as tore up as they could.

Every weekend Black came home drunk.

And I knew he drank. Just ain't ever seen him pissy drunk like he was. Speech slurred, stumblin' over the lil bit of furniture that was in the house. He'd come home all times of the night. Well, when he did come home, do whatever in that bed, then be so dead in sleep his snores could wake up the neighborhood.

I was mad at myself for not thinkin' things through.

When he was home, he might as well had been out hangin' with his friends. Ain't like he help much. He sat around while I did everythin'. Cooked, cleaned where I could, get the kids together, tiptoed around Lily, who really ain't like me much. Despite me trying to make the most of it, everything just seemed harder than I expected it to be.

And I couldn't believe Black ain't have them kids in school.

Six kids and Black never thought they deserved education. Even I had a lil bit of schoolin' behind me. Made sense why I'd see Lily and Pinky on the porch durin' the day when they should've been elsewhere.

Lily and Pinky, at eight and ten, had their routine down pat. Started to feel like I wasn't needed and I'm sure it was intentional, but I ain't blame her none. They'd been without their mama for so long, and with Black being everywhere but where he was 'posed to be, Lily becomin' the mama of the house made sense.

I felt the power struggle between her and me.

I believe she thought I was comin' in to take over or maybe even replace her mama, but that wasn't my intent. Never really got a chance to tell her that.

Black had 'dem kids workin' for some sharecropper down the road. Ain't even have time to make 'em breakfast some days, which wasn't much. They'd be up and out before the sun even touched the sky, headin' over to pick cotton and tobacco. The girls picked cotton and the boys picked tobacco. Dem boys made a lil more than the girls since tobacco was becomin' more popular with the older folks. Couldn't even afford no smokes or a cigar, but we was out here pickin' tobacco for it.

They did ten hour shifts and was home by mid-afternoon. Didn't have much to cook and Black ain't leave no money, so I had to go out back and see what I could find. That yard was no different than the trail I'd walk to school. Was able to pick up a few weeds and mushrooms for some stew. Some days I'd have to swallow my pride and kill a squirrel runnin' in the back. After the first few times, it ain't bother me much. Just became the thing to do. Mr. Shepard would sneak and leave some lemons at the back door, and I'd make lemonade so the kids had something else to drink beside water.

One time I tried to set the table like we did at Uncle Willie's, but that ain't go over too well. Most times they'd go back and forth between settin' at the table, eatin' on the floor or pilin' up in that small room of theirs.

Every day before they ate supper, Lily would collect all the money and place it in a box in the room where Black and I slept. Wasn't too comfortable with her going in the room so freely, or even knowin' his drawers the way she did. Made it seem like it was her room just as much as it was mine. Wanted to say somethin', but I really ain't want no trouble with Black's kids, so I let it go. Didn't see no point in tryin' to change up what they already had.

The rest of the kids moved on Lily's accord. When she got herself ready to eat, they'd get themselves in order, washed their hands and faces, then sat to the table. I'd fix their plates and they'd all look at Lily to see if she was gon eat first. I realized then that they wouldn't eat if she ain't like it and they'd rather starve than cross their sister. Ain't never seen no child have a hold on their siblings like she did hers.

One afternoon after they got home from workin', I made a squirrel stew and added a few grains of rice I found in the cabinet. They did their usual routine, then set to the table and waited to be served. I'd start with Lily first 'cause she was the oldest, then Pinky and move down the line. Once I'd served them all, I stood back to see their reaction. If Lily ain't like it, then I'd have huge pot of stew I'd have to throw out back. Black rarely ate what the kids had, so I had to cook different for him.

I watched her pick up the spoon, look over at me, then the plate.

"You git this out back?" she asked. "Yes." I replied a lil anxious. I ain't think about what they'd eat if she ain't like it. You'd think by this time I'd have a backup plan but I never did.

She sniffed the spoon, stuck the tip of her tongue inside the liquid, then patted her lips together like she was tastin' for somethin'. Felt like we was all holdin' our breath to see what she was gon do or say.

"Ya'll can eat." She spoke, then took another slurp of the stew.

I watched them all inhale it in a matter of minutes then get up and have seconds and thirds. Of all the stuff I made, it was safe to say they liked that best, so it's what I'd make in the afternoon when they came back from work. In the evening, I'd cook some type of meat I could find, with some gravy and potatoes I'd borrow from Ms. Ann.

She was our neighbor to the right of us, which was still a long way down the road when you walkin.

I'd always smell those cakes she made. I'd want to ask her for some for the kids. It'd be just my luck Black come home one of those days and I'd have to explain where I got it from, 'cause we ain't had no money to get no fancy cakes like that.

As much as Lily made it seem like she was hard to please, her and the kids were the easiest to cook for. Black was the challenge. He'd always want breakfast and dinner prepared a certain way, which I found hard to do since we barely had food. I wondered if he realized we were poor, or just like to pretend he lived like a king.

Our house looked like some old beat up shed

on a farm.

We were the only shack on the street and I wanted to be embarrassed, but I just held it all in for the kids. I knew if I felt embarrassed, the kids had to feel worse, 'cause they lived there all they lives. When I did have the courage to ask him for money, he'd only give me $20. That wasn't near enough to cover a month's worth food and clothes for seven people. He'd take the money the kids made and pocket it. I asked one time what he did with it and that turned to an argument where he raised his hand at me. It was the last time I questioned him about the money.

I didn't know who Black was anymore.

Or…

maybe I just never knew him at all.

That sweet and caring man I'd met years ago became a distant memory. In a blink of an eye, he'd turned into a mean ol' grinch. I was so naive then that it didn't make sense. Years later a woman named Maya Angelou said, "When people show you who they are, believe them." I sure wish someone woulda said that earlier, although I'm still not sure if it woulda changed things.

While Black and I was courting, I remember someone from the church say he was shell-shock from the war. I ain't know what that meant and wasn't sure if how he treated me and the kids had somethin' to do with it. There were nights I'd stare at him mumblin' in his sleep. Sometimes even fightin', sayin' names of people I ain't never heard of. One evening he screamed so loud from whatever was gettin' at him in his sleep, the kids came runnin' in the room, scared somethin' happened. I had Lily heat 'em up some warm milk to calm his nerves.

First time I seen Black look afraid.

I reached out to grab him, comfort him, and he pushed me away, yelled at the kids to go back to sleep and walked into the kitchen. I stayed up to wait for him to come back to bed, but I must've fallen asleep 'cause when I woke up, he was gone and so were the kids.

Ain't had no clue who this man was that slept next to me, what he was dreamin' 'bout or the thoughts in his head. Had this fancy notion that marriage was 'posed to bring us all close together, but all it did was create this space that I ain't know how to fill.

And he hardly said a word to the kids.

They'd stay in their room or play outside when he was around. Never realized there was this distance between them. When they reach to hug 'em, he'd push them off. Tell 'em to go sit they asses down somewhere. They'd look at him, then at me and run which would set Black off. So he'd chase 'em 'round the house tryin' to beat 'em somthin awful. Lookin' back on it now, that's probably why he never brought me 'round. Prolly knew I'd have a change of heart if I really knew how he was livin' or treatin' dem kids.

I'd suggest we do things as a family, like catch a movie in town or have a day at the park. He always said no, claimin' he was tired and wanted to keep his weekends to himself. I knew it was an excuse and the kids did too, but they wouldn't dare question Black 'cause he'd put a whippin' on them so hard it hurt me. Had me wonderin' if he beat dem kids like that all the time.

Sooner than later, I got the answer to that question.

One night Elijah asked if Black could take the boys out fishin' and he refused again. Chile, Dennis must've been feelin' himself that day 'cause he fussed back at Black.

"We never go anywhere daddy!" He yelled.

Dennis folded his arms, tears waterin' up in his eyes, skin all red and flushed. You could hear a pin drop in that room.

It was unnervin'.

Black sat on this big cloth chair, the most expensive thing in that house, sippin' on a beer, the case by the foot of the couch. He just sat there and sipped. Eyes fixed on that dusty fireplace that barely struck a fire. His face blank. I looked at Dennis and motioned for him to go in the room, but before he could move, Black was on his behind beatin' him with those large, thick, lumberjack hands.

"Black stop!" I screamed, but it ain't help much. His hands moved up and down on Dennis' body so much it looked like a blur. "He's sorry Black, stop. You ain't gotta beat 'em like that."

I tried to pull him off Dennis, but he just kept beatin' 'em, like there was no end in sight.

Dennis screamed so loud he lost his voice. All the kids stood and watched Black beat Dennis like he stole somethin'. In a desperate attempt, I climbed on his back and tried to grab his hand. I dunno what the heck was on my mind when I did that.

He threw me cross the room with one hand. "Woman you betta get the hell off me!" He yelled. I flew back into the wall near the fireplace.

Lily and Pinky ran over to me, while Elijah and Charlie Jr. slid behind Dennis to drag him from under Black's hand. If Black was gonna beat one of us, he was gonna have to beat all us that night. I'd never been so afraid in my life, not since that mule almost attacked me.

Shoot, in that moment, he was the mule, his eyes bloodshot.

I blamed it on the fact that he might be drunk and slept in the kids' room that night just in case he had another episode.

Wishful thinkin'.

"Roxie!"

Black's screams could be heard down the road. I hoped the kids were asleep but two of 'em were up just as I.

"Roxie! Woman, I know you hear me callin'

you!"

Figured if I'd played sleep, maybe he'd go back in his room and sleep all that alcohol off, but again, wishful thinkin'.

We were all crowded on that small behind bed, all seven of us. Lily, Pinky and Sarah slept head to foot to the right of me. I placed myself in the middle with the thought to be a shield. The boys mixed themselves up to the left of me, at my feet and under my arm.

Lily and Dennis were awake.

They were both at the foot of the bed. I could feel 'em shiftin' 'round, movin' close to one 'nother, tryin' to lock their arms and legs together, like a puzzle piece. It was then I realized, this ain't new to them, it's normal. Their normal.

Black's footsteps were wobbly but close.

I could see his shadow inchin' closer to the door. I whispered the Lord's Prayer while the kids scrunched up closer to me. Before I got the last verse out, he buss through the door.

"Roxie, get 'cho ass up! I know you heard me callin' you!"

The kids pushed themselves so close to me I could smell their breath. His steps were still off balance. Hoped he'd just fall and hit the floor in a drunken stupor, but again, wishful thinkin'.

He reached over Charlie Jr. who was locked onto my feet, grabbed me by neck and held me in the air. Elijah reached to pull me down and he slapped him into the wall. All of them screamed for him to let me go. Charlie refused to let go of my feet and Black dragged the both of us out the bed and into the hallway. He squeezed harder, danglin' me like a ragdoll. I could feel life leavin' me with each breath I tried to take.

"Charlie, if you don't take yo ass back in that room, I'll kill 'er." His fingertips pressed deeper in my throat, the air goin' down thinner. "You want that on yo conscience boy? Huh? You want that?"

He taunted Charlie.

That boy was too scared to let me go and too scared to hold on.

He whimpered. "No."

"No what!"

"No, sir."

55

"Then take yo hands off her legs and get back in that room, NOW!"

He hesitated, then moved his hands from my ankles, tears streamin' down his face, the horror in his eyes, knowin' what was to come. I was more afraid for him than me. I hated them to see this. All of 'em. We all knew this was wrong, but there was nothin' we could do without one of us gettin' killed.

"It's OK baby." My words came choppy with me tryin' to preserve whatever breath I had left. "It's OK. I'll be alright. Go on to bed, K?"

He cried.

Slow draggin' back to the room, his head turnin' back 'round to me in each step. The more he dragged, the tighter Black's grip was on my neck. "Keep wastin' time boy and she gon die tonight."

Charlie looked back at him.

I could see the anger and hurt in his eyes, feeling helpless. He wasn't but five years old, but no one could tell 'em that he wasn't no man. He hurried back and closed the door. I could hear the sobs, tryna hold it in, but scared Black would go back on his word and kill me anyway.

Life Ain't Been No Crystal Stair

At this point, I'm sure he was good for it.

His kids never called me mama, but that night, I was. I protected them as best I could, just like any mama would.

"And stay in there until it's time to get up for breakfast." He paused. "I swear to God if any of ya'll come out that room before the sun come up, I'll wear your narrow behinds out!"

Black loosened his grip on my neck, but kept me in the air until we got back to his room. He threw me on the bed and began to unbuckle his pants.

"You think you slick huh? Like I wouldn't come find you."

His raspy voice pained my ears.

I feared him.

There was nothin' attractive about Black, and I thought of how to get myself out this situation. He slid onto the bed and in me. As he pushed himself inside me, sweatin', droolin' from the drunkenness, his breath hot on my skin, moanin' like an injured horse. At that point, I accepted there was no out.

I pushed my hands up against his shoulders

trying to create space between him and me, and he grabbed my wrists. I flinched and cried. I tried to scream but he bit my lip until the skin broke. The wetness slidin' down the inside of my mouth. Black only lasted a few minutes, but this time it felt like hours. I needed a prayer, a verse, somethin' to comfort me and I remembered 2 Corinthians 1:3-4.

Blessed be God, the Father of our Lord Jesus Christ, the Father of mercies, and the God of all comfort, who comforts us in all our tribulation, that we may be able to comfort those who are in any trouble by the comfort with which we ourselves are comforted by God.

I whispered it to myself and Black bit my lip harder. His rough movements mashed my head 'gainst the wall since we ain't had no headboard. My head mashed up 'gainst the wall so hard, I blacked out still whisperin' the God's words in my mind.

The next morning, I woke up to him passed out on top of me. He was so heavy, it took every ounce of strength I had left to get him to roll over. The girls peeked into the room to see if he was still sleep. They looked at me, and I back at them. Lily walked away from the door and headed to the furnace to heat up water for a bath. Soon as I stepped my toe on the floor, he grumbled, movin' about on the bed. The girls and I froze, scared he'd jump up and kill us, but all he did was turn over on his stomach, his sweat and musk seepin' through the sheets.

I moved as fast as I could with the girls and into the bathroom. They helped me in the tub and got breakfast ready while I washed the nastiness off me. Leavin' wasn't an option. As much as I wanted to try for the kids, I couldn't see it happenin'.

Later on that day, while the kids were gone and Black was still sleep, I stopped over to Uncle Willie's house. I was surprised to see Cousin Sara. Hadn't seen her since she left to move to the Big City. Soon as they saw my split lip, Uncle Willie went to load his shotgun, but I begged him not to. I couldn't have no more trouble goin' on in that house. The kids and I had to live with him, not Uncle Willie and 'nem. 'Gainst his better judgement he ain't go after Black, but begged me to take the kids back to Birmingham with Sara. I knew this had to be a sign from God, but I was scared. There's no way an out could be that simple, 'cause if it was, I woulda been took the kids and left, even though they wasn't mine to take.

Sara was leaving the next day and said we could get tickets at the station.

She was confident we'd be fine and I could get work out there for the kids. My heart pumped so fast. The thought of sneakin' out and leavin' with the kids scared me. What if Black saw us and shot us all? What if he followed us to the train station and shot up the station? I hated riskin' everyone else on my behalf.

"Roxie, please give it some thought." She pleaded. "This is ain't no way to be livin'. You don't have any kids wit him. You deserve better. Let his drunk self live alone. Please consider leavin' wit me tomorrow."

I stared at her and Uncle Willie. "I'll think about it." I paused. "Just not sure if now is the right time."

"So when is the right time!" Uncle Willie yelled. "When he kill you? Cause then it's too late."

"I know Uncle Willie, I know."

"So let us help you." He sighed. "I know me and yo Aunt ain't really been there for you and I'm sorry, but this ain't no way to live. Let us help you."

"I'll think about it." I grabbed the soft cloth pouch I carry 'round and headed out the door. "The kids'll be home soon, I gotta get their stew started."

Life Ain't Been No Crystal Stair

I hugged both Sara and Uncle Willie, then left. The walk home wasn't long enough for me to think it through, so I stayed with the decision to leave on my mind while I fixed the stew and got the wood together for the furnace. Black was gone when I got there but the kids were home. I hurried up and got the stew ready. I was lucky enough to get some flour and eggs while Black wasn't 'round, so I made some biscuits and put those in the oven while I cooked the stew. I had a few wood chips left, but knew I'd had to get more wood to make dinner.

Once their lunch was done, the kids ate and kept to themselves. Lily and I kept lockin' eyes but I wasn't sure if she was tryin' to tell me somethin' or just felt bad about what happened.

A few hours later Black came back and sat at his chair with his beers. We didn't have TV, so he'd listen to some folks talkin' on the radio. I'd tried to understand what they was sayin' so Black and I had somethin' to talk about, but I couldn't figure it out. Some type of news show, nothin' entertanin' that all us could listen to.

I begged Black to get us some chicken 'cause I got tired of makin' coon and squirrel. He fussed wit me, but was sure to bring back the smallest chicken he could find. It frustrated me so, but I had to make due and hope it fed us all.

I was willin' to skip a meal so all the kids could eat.

I only had so much flour, so I ain't make no more biscuits. Found some more long grain rice packed up in the back of the cabinet. Then I wondered what other food might be hidden 'round the house.

I used the rice, made some gravy with the bit of flour I had left and prepared the chicken. Black sat to the table first and all the kids stood there while I fixed his plate. When his plate was done, the kids fixed their own plate. Lily, Pinky and Sarah sat on the floor and the boys sat to the table with Black. I stood by the oven and sipped on a glass of water. All seemed well, but Black stared at his plate and wouldn't touch a bite.

"Black. You alright?"

I looked at him and I noticed that blank stare. The same stare he had last night before he beat Dennis and I was nervous. He's never complained about the food, so I wasn't sure what to think.

"Yo food gonna get cold if you don't eat it

Black."

The kids looked at me, and I back at them. Everyone grabbed their plates and headed into the room. They moved with haste while Black continued to stare into space with that blank look.

"Black."

"Woman I heard you the first time." He looked down at his plate, picked up his fork and swirled it around his plate. "I don't like it."

"You sure? You didn't even taste —"

"I told you I don't like it!"

I jumped.

I could hear the kids tellin' each other to keep quiet. I took a deep breath and thought about what I would say next so I could avoid gettin' hit.

"OK. What would you like instead?"

"Not this mess. It's late. Whatchu gon' cook now this late?"

"Black, I can make somethin'."

"I don't want what you got to cook. I spent my money on this chicken and this all you could do with it?

"Black this all we —"

"I don't give a damn about what we got in here! You tryna say we poor? That we ain't got enough food? That I don't provide for this family?" He got up from the table and tossed the chicken on the floor then poured the pitcher of lemonade over it. "And where the hell you get lemons to make lemonade? Got you some man givin' you and my kids food?"

"No Black."

"If I catch you lyin' Roxie, that's yo ass! Now clean this mess up off the floor."

I watched him walk out the door and I held back tears. All the kids accept Lily came out to help me clean up.

"It's OK ya'll. I got it. Get ready for bed."

I looked over to see Lily standing in the hall. We caught eyes and she walked back to the room. It didn't take me as long to clean up the mess, but if I needed a sign that it was time to go, this was it.

While they slept, I packed whatever I could in a few suitcases I had when I moved and got myself ready. I snuck over to Uncle Willie's and he agreed to come get me take and take me to the train station. I ain't want to leave the kids but they wasn't mine to take.

The next mornin', Uncle Willie was outside waitin' for me. I hadn't even gotten the kids up. I looked out the window and he motioned for me to come on but I couldn't. Just ain't feel right; couldn't leave those kids. I looked down the road and saw Black comin' down the street. I kissed the inside of my hand, put it to the window, and walked away. I placed the suitcases behind the dresser in the kids' room so he wouldn't notice. Black came in the house, headed to the room, grabbed new clothes and left.

I knew I'd missed my opportunity to leave.

My fear kept me from being free from a man who ain't never meant to do me no good.

I sat at the kitchen table and cried.

Even with the kids around I still felt alone. I looked up and Lily was standin' there lookin' at me, as if she knew what I wanted to do, as if she was waitin' for me to just up and leave like her mama. We locked eyes again and she walked away, unbothered by whatever emotion I was feelin', and in her own way, told me to get over it 'cause whatever I was thinkin', whatever I was tryna plan, it just wasn't gonna happen.

I hated knowin' she was right.

Chapter Six

Lily

She was a pretty girl, but no one would ever notice 'cause she was so scraggly. Had this petite shape and fine, curly hair that always looked nappy 'cause it was hardly ever combed. I could tell Brenda tried to do somethin' wit it, but it never lasted long. Pinky and Sarah had more thick, coarse hair, so his sister would braid theirs easily. It was like she was the red-headed stepchild that everyone dismissed.

Lily.

Black's eldest daughter, who always seemed like she was against me somedays. Could never tell if she hated me or the life Black made her and her siblings live. Before we got married, I'd walk past the house to see her and Pinky outside playin'. She'd always stop and stare. She knew me and her father was seein' each other, but I couldn't tell whether she liked me or not. Pinky would wave and speak, but never Lily. She'd just give this stare that felt like her eyes were lookin' right through me. Like she saw what was about to happen before it happened.

Maybe she did.

After Black and I came from the courthouse, she helped moved my things into the room where he and I would sleep, and noticed how familiar she was wit the space. At the time, I ain't think much of it. That night, she helped wit dinner and I saw she knew how to keep a house. She already had a routine wit her brothers and sisters, so I'd try and find other ways to get to know her. We had this silent agreement that she'd handle her siblings and I'd take care of the rest.

And it worked.

I couldn't get her to say more than two words to me, but she kept the rest of the chil'ren in line. As nervous as I was, I'd hope things would fall into place, but my hope was short lived.

This one weekend, Black woke up so excited. It was odd 'cause I wasn't used to him being this happy, but I figured maybe he had a good week at work. He decided to have us visit his mother, so we hopped in the car and drove a few miles down the road to see Ms. Beulah. She was always nice to me and she loved her kids, all her kids.

It was cool for a summer day and the sun was bright in the sky. No clouds. I sat in the front while the kids piled themselves up in the back. We got to Ms. Beulah's and she came out to greet us. I got out to help the kids and noticed the car still runnin' with Lily in it, but I paid it no mind. The rest of us walked to the porch and when I turn 'round, Black and Lily were gone. Before I could question anythin', Ms. Beulah's soft voice brought me back to reality.

"Why don't ya'll come inside. I got some sweet potato pie in the oven that's almost ready."

The kids ran in house and I stared at the road wonderin' why they drove off and ain't come inside. Ms. Beulah came back out and tapped me on the shoulder. Finally, I walked in confused, not sure what to think. The kids were at the table eatin' pie and Ms. Beulah looked at me like she wanted to say somethin', but she just smiled and fixed me some sweet tea.

I didn't say much while we were there.

Two hours later, Black came back to pick up me and the kids without Lily. We'd been there so long, Ms. Beulah had us eat dinner with her so the kids wouldn't be hungry when we got back.

I looked at Black. "Where'd you go, and where's Lily?" I paused and checked the back to make sure the kids were all in.

"Why you worrin' bout what I do wit my daughter?"

"I ain't tryna fuss wit you Black. Just ain't know you was takin' Lily anywhere. Was 'spectin' all us to be wit Ms. Beulah."

"Agin, why you worrin' bout what I do wit my daughter?"

I took a breath cause I ain't want no trouble. "The kids and I already ate with Ms. Beulah."

"Good, that means you can cook enough dinner just for me."

I took another breath, then glanced back at the kids and sat quiet on the way to the house. I didn't bother to ask where Lily was because I knew she was home. Still, I was curious to where they went. I ain't understand why he wanted to separate us. When we got home, I saw her curled up like a ball in the bed. I wondered if she was sick. I went to check on her, but Black fussed wantin' me to fix dinner. Pinky and Sarah made her bath like they knew what was wrong. The boys went in the room and closed the door. I couldn't figure out what happened, so I fixed Black his food.

I made a cornish hen, a nice and fat one.

Checked the icebox to see if he'd bought more, but there was only one for him. It bothered me how selfish he was.

There was this unsettlin' feeling in my spirit, so I had a mind to take the kids to church the next day. We ain't go often, but that feelin' in my spirit had me believe it was needed.

The girls finished with Lily, so I cleaned out the tub and got his bath ready. Once he was done, he went on to the bathroom. While he took his bath. I cleaned up the kitchen, put fresh sheets on the bed and prepared to go to sleep. Black came out the bathroom with no shirt on, just his pants, then changed when he got in the room. He had that look in his eye and I wasn't sure if he was about to have one of his episodes. The kids had the door cracked after they'd gotten Lily together, so I made eyes with them to closed the door all the way.

He touched the cotton with the tips of his fingers, takin' in the feel of the cloth.

"You put fresh sheets on the bed?"

"Yes." I hesitated.

"Good." He smiled. "You can gon on and sleep on the couch tonight."

"What for?"

"What I tell you about questionin' me Roxie! I ain't got time for you sassin' me tonight. Do as I say!"

"I just...fine Black." I headed to living room. "I'll be nice." He called out. "You can sleep in my chair."

My heart sank.

I couldn't figure out what I'd done to make him want me in the living room. That unsettlin' feelin' grew stronger. Soon it became a knot in the pit of my stomach. It was too strong to let go and I knew me tryna be brave again would get me beat, but

Life Ain't Been No Crystal Stair

I just had to know. Soon as I got up the courage to ask what I did wrong, I heard a knock at the kids' door.

That knot in my stomach almost came up my throat. I ain't know what to think, so I went back to the chair, grabbed the blanket I brought from Uncle Willie and Aunt Martha's and closed my eyes. I didn't want to assume things, so I convinced myself it was all in my mind.

Until the next mornin' when I saw the girls bringin' Lily to the bathroom, just like they did the day before, I almost threw up on the floor. The thought of Black seein' it, knowin' I assumed he did wrong and gettin' beat, stopped me.

Still, just couldn't get over the thoughts runnin' through my mind.

Those thoughts alone was enough for me.

Black came in the kitchen, smirked at me, then sat at the table and waited for his breakfast. "Sleep well?" He taunted. He smirked that slick grin and looked at me hopin' I'd say somethin' so he could slap me clean 'cross the room. Just the act of me questionin' him and makin' 'sumptions, I ain't no nothin' 'bout was enough reasonin' for 'em. I kept my thoughts to myself, and my head down while I fixed his juice like normal and got breakfast ready.

"I'm gon take the kids to church today."

There was silence, then he cleared his throat. "Well, you can't stay long 'cause I'm meetin' with Ricky this afternoon for cards. So ya'll betta pray to God for twenty minutes and be outside, or ya'lls be walkin' back to da house." He waited for me to respond, hopin' I'd just cancel so he wouldn't be bothered. "You heard me?"

"Yes Black." I paused. "I heard you."

Lily peeked in the kitchen.

We caught eyes and she greeted me with that stare that pierced every part of my skin. It was a stare that I became familiar with. Hoped each time her and I caught eyes, that she'd see my sorrow, the pain for not being able to do more for her, but she didn't and that hurt me.

I hated feelin' helpless.

I was failin' these kids. I knew they wasn't mine to worry 'bout, but the person in me couldn't just dismiss 'em and focus on myself. Not when we all share the same nightmare. Me not being able to protect them the way I thought I should wore on me. I had no idea I married a monster and there was nothin' I could do to fix it. I would've never thought Black would be sleepin' with any of his girls. There were so many women I knew he messed 'round wit. Couldn't understand what he'd want wit his own daughter.

By the time I caught on to what he was doing, she was eleven.

When she got older, I found out he'd been keepin' up wit her since she was real young. There were many nights I was made to sleep outside the room, while he did whatever to her. And I'm sure a part of her hoped that once he married me it would stop, but it didn't.

Three years into the marriage, I got pregnant with my first girl. While that baby was in me, I'd be called out the room to that "magical" chair, and what life was left in that girl was gone.

I never got used to him callin' her to his bed.

The older she got, the worse her attitude got. Didn't matter how much she told people what Black was doin' to her, no one believed it.

She even told Ms. Beulah.

Ms. Beulah called that girl a liar and told her to stop spreadin' rumors 'bout her son. I was too afraid to back up her stories, fearful Black would kill me and the kids. Lily barely talked to me but that stare said all the words she refused to say.

And he was never outright with it.

The secrecy 'bout it made me believe he knew it was wrong, but did it just 'cause he could and couldn't no one beat 'em, or wasn't brave enough to try.

When she was thirteen, she started puttin' up a lil fight, which would piss Black off. Lily wasn't the same young girl he used to force himself on. She had some weight on her and was very shapely. Her body made him lust after her more. By the time she was fifteen, they were almost fist fightin'. As much as he'd overpower her, she wouldn't let him get on her without a fight.

It was another drunk Saturday night for Black and torture for Lily, but this night was a lil different... even for him.

"Get off me!" She screamed.

I'd hear them tusslin' and want to help, but I

was so scared. Decidin' to let us all live and him have his way broke my heart even more. I just didn't have the fight in me to risk the kids' lives and mine. I knew I couldn't overpower Black, no matter how angry I was. And I knew, in his crazy mind, he thought I was jealous, but there's no way I could've been jealous of what he did to her.

No woman in her right mind would be.

The tusslin' continued, so I put the radio on to drown out the noise, then went to check on the kids. The girls were in tears when I got to the room. The boys, all three of 'em, were sittin' straight up like they was 'bout to rush in there and end it. I tried to tuck 'em in, settle 'em down.

They jumped at my touch.

It was hot in that room. The air was so thick, right along with the emotions. I could barely breathe and wondered how they managed. I opened the window, said the Our Father over them and closed the door.

The next mornin', I went to get the kids up for breakfast and church. When I came 'round to the rooms, Black had his tore all the way up. The bed was turn over, clothes out the drawers, lamp broken on the floor. Couldn't figure out where all that was comin' from until I went in the kids' room and saw the drawer where Lily kept her clothes empty. Everything gone, along with her shoes.

She'd left.

I never envied Lily. I never wanted to be her, but in that moment, I wished I was. I wished I had the nerve to get up and leave wit my kids and his.

That was the only time I ever wanted to be Lily.

Chapter Seven

Buttermilk

It was 1952 when Lily left. By that time, I had my first four children with Black. Marley, Angela, Brenda and Irma who came a few months after Lily left. Black had no idea where she went, but I had a mind she went to stay with some family out in Florida.

With her gone, I was scared Black might start messin' with his other girls, but I got lucky, at least I think I did. He just kept me pregnant and beat us all while he went out and did whatever. Since he ain't touch none of the other girls, I knew he was gettin' it from somewhere else. Just ain't know who and hoped it wasn't another young girl like Lily.

It was getting crowded with all the kids and I begged Black to get us a bigger house, but all he did was buy more beds and tell me to make due. We had nine kids in the house. He bought bunk beds to put in that tiny behind room and threatened to whip the eldest ones if they even thought about sleeping in 'em. I wasn't comfortable with the small ones on them bunk beds, but what Black says goes, so that's where they slept.

He never really beat the kids we had together, but he'd go all in on the rest of us. Doubt he cared about his first set of kids. Wondered if there was some resentment 'cause their mama left. He wasn't quite as cruel to mine as he was to the others, but he wasn't the nicest either. Wasn't like he gave mine the world, although, it was a piece of the world the others ain't get.

I'm sure they wondered why they were treated so cruel.

'Bout a few months after I had Angela in '49, Uncle Willie and Aunt Martha moved to Birmingham with the rest of my mother's family. Once they left, I knew there was no out. Ain't even get a chance to say goodbye. They were much older, and since I was dealin' with Black's mess, Sarah and the rest of my cousins couldn't leave their care up to chance.

Right before my fifth child in '54, a few of my uncles passed one after the other. With them gone, Black's drunken mind thought Sarah was the only family I had left besides my own kids. I'm sure his intent was to make it so I ain't have nobody to run to, and he knew I wouldn't involve anyone else.

Made me hate him more.

He knew it, but he ain't care.

Black's kids were almost grown, and a lot bigger than they were when we first married, especially the boys. He'd come at Elijah and Charlie Jr. and it'd almost be a bloodbath with them fightin' in the street. I almost lost one of the babies tryna to break up fights between him and the boys.

A few years after Lily left Pinky ran away to Florida with some of Black's people and a few years after that Sarah left too. Luckily Black didn't spect nothin or he would've tried to kill'em just for havin a mind to leave. I don't blame those children for leavin. Living with Black was a nightmare. There was plenty of nights Pinky would run away and sleep in the woods. I often worried about the youngest one Sarah. She reminded me so much of Lily and I prayed to GOD that Black wasn't doing to her what he had done to Lily but I suspect that he was.

Once all the girls was gone my beatings got worse.

He beat me so bad.

I'd plead for Ms. Beulah and the family to help me and the kids, but they never did. They hated that Black beat on us, but never leant a helpin' hand. No one ever said anythin' to 'em, not even Lula, who wouldn't do nothin' but mock me saying, I shouldn't've married no man old enough to be my daddy in the first place.

Black's family couldn't help me even if they wanted to. Blood is thicker than water as they say.

I thought havin' my fifth child would be easy, but she was a rough one. I had all my babies at home 'cause Black was too cheap to pay for a hospital room, so I had the same midwife since Marley.

Of all my kids, Brenda was the lightest. I had no idea where her skin color came from, and Black immediately accused me of cheatin'. It was funny 'cause there were rumors 'round town of him fatherin' chil'ren from other women. Years later, I found out a member of the church had Black's son same day I had one of mine. Despite his false 'spicions, he ain't never treat her like she wasn't his.

That same year, Elijah, Charlie Jr. and Dennis had moved from pullin' tobacco, to plowin' the fields at another sharecropper's farm. He was colored. Wasn't sure how he managed to get that farm, but he had the respect from most people in town.

Mr. Tulman.

He always tried to get the boys to bring home some of the crops they help harvest, but they always refused. They knew their daddy wouldn't do nothin' but toss it back out in the street, or stomp on it out of jealousy. 'Dem boys was old enough to help provide good for the house, but Black was so jealous of any other man havin' control, all he did was continue to steal they money and challenge 'em to fights. I knew one day dem boys would either kill Black or just leave like the rest.

That time came sooner than later.

It was dead in the middle of summer and the

humidity was startin' to pick up. That day, the boys came home and ain't have no money to put in that box Black kept under the floorboard in his room.

They went straight to they own room and closed the door.

I got nervous 'cause Black kept count of what each of 'em made per week. He'd use that money and go into town with his friends and their wives, get drunk, play cards, then run around with his other women. I'd thought by now, the kids felt like they could tell me anythin', but I figure they ain't want me to know and risk gettin' beat.

I understood that.

Charlie Jr. came out the room to the bathroom and stared at me. I could tell somethin' was on his mind, but I ain't wanna press it. Really, I ain't need to cause he came out wit it like a faucet. "Mama...we leavin' soon." Elijah and Dennis ran out their room and almost tackled him.

"CJ! We agreed not to tell her 'till we had all the money from Mr. Tulman." Dennis yelled and grit his teeth.

"I got the money." He paused. "All of it."

Charlie Jr. looked at them, back at me, then went to the bathroom.

My heart fluttered.

Wasn't sure if it was 'cause they'd made a plan to leave and it was happenin' or 'cause it left me alone with Black and six kids.

"When it's time, let me know and I'll make you some biscuits for the road." They could see my face was sad, but we all knew they couldn't stay.

"Mama." Charlie walked out from the bathroom. "Ain't no need to do all that."

"Maybe we can sneak some food by?" Dennis cut in.

"Yeah." Elijah replied. "You know, since Mr. Tulman always tryna give us stuff. Wouldn't last that long, but it could hold you over for 'bout a week or so." He looked at me and cracked a half smile.

"Whatever you boys feel is best. I'm grateful either way."

They reach over and hugged me. That moment of bondin' was short lived when Black walked in the house fussin'.

"So this what ya'll do when I'm at work? Try and hump on Roxie?" He stormed to the back loosenin' the belt from his pants. "Dis what ya'll do when I'm at work? When I ain't 'round?"

I walked passed Black. "Dis ain't what you thinkin' Black. Let dem boys alone. They worked hard today."

"And I don't!?"

Black drew his hand back and Dennis stood in between us. "And what the hell you gon do?" Black's smirk mocked his bravery. He gazed to his left and saw Elijah and Charlie Jr. were already in position to take 'em out if necessary.

"I see Roxie got ya'll real tough in here."

Him and Dennis stayed locked in that stare. I moved into the kitchen outta harm's way and motioned for the lil' ones to close the door.

"What you gon do boy?" Black continued to mock him. Dennis balled up his fist. His face was blank, but I could see the anger lingerin'. It's the same look Lily had, no more cares, ready to deal with whatever was to come from the challenge, 'cause they all knew there was something harsh comin.

Elijah tried to talk him down, but he stood firm. I knew it was his way of telling Black he wasn't afraid no more. And he wasn't no scrawny man. All three boys were muscular, but Dennis was bigger than Black in size and just a few inches under him, and Black wasn't no short man. That stare down between them felt like hours.

"Oh! Now I ain't worth this fake ass whopin' you 'posed to give me?"

Dennis glanced him up and down, then turned back to the room. Black lunged at him and Elijah slid in front of Dennis before Black could land the blow. He gave Black that same stare, went back in the room and closed the door. "Everybody think they tough 'round here but don't do nuthin' for dis house!" He fussed. I went back to the kitchen to finish gettin' dinner ready, but I knew someone had to catch all that rage. I knew he was finna beat me just 'cause.

"And you think just 'cause dem boys 'round you can sass me!"

He stomped around the kitchen, slammin' his hand on the table, bangin' up against the walls. There was a rifle on the side of the sink and I wasn't sure if he was gon shoot me. I tried to keep calm and continued cuttin' up the potatoes for the stew. He mushed his hands up against my head. Teasin' me, yellin' loud enough for the lil ones to hear, mad cause I wouldn't give him a reason to beat me, which set 'em off more, 'cause I wouldn't give in.

"So you just gon stand there and not say nothin'! Huh!?" His hands became a rhythm up 'gainst my head that I continued to ignore. "Huh!? Nothin' Roxie, NOTHIN'!?" My neck started to get stiff. I squeezed the knife in my hand, sweat gatherin' up between my fingers, drippin' under my arms and on my forehead.

I went back and forth over whether to just stab him and fire the rifle, but then I remembered I ain't no how to shoot and Black would kill me.

I couldn't leave my babies.

I couldn't mess up the boy's chance to leave.

Black's musty breath was on my skin causin' me to sweat more. I choked on every tear I swallowed, but a few made it down my face. My head tipped so far over from the force, I tripped over my feet and the knife slid out my hand. Black caught it, wrapped his forearm around my neck and placed the knife right at the side of my throat. The thought of me bein' frightened, knowin' that he could end my life in seconds, excited him.

I felt how much it excited him.

His choppy breath pierced my skin, "If you don't wanna speak, fine. I'll just slit yo throat and save you the trouble of actin' like you can't." The knife slowly punctured my skin. I jumped from the sensation of my blood drippin' down my neck. "Still gon act like you can't speak?" He kept mockin' me.

I couldn't move.

The more he pressed his body up against mine, slidin' the tip of the knife 'cross my throat, the more nauseous I got. Even felt a lil pee drip down my legs. I couldn't speak even if I wanted to, cause his grip 'round my neck was so tight, I could barely utter a sound.

Black was so busy tryin' to keep that fear in my heart, that he ain't hear the light pitter-patter behind him.

"Daddy! Let mama go, daddy! Let her go! You hurtin' mama daddy!" Irma's soft voice rang out through the house. I heard Marley's voice trying to get her back in the room, but Irma was feisty. She wasn't but three years old, and feisty as a mule.

"Go back in the room now!" Black yelled.

"No Daddy! You hurtin' mama!"

I could hear the tears in her voice.

"You gon kill me in front of yo daughter?" I murmured.

Kept my body still 'cause I couldn't tell what he was gon do.

Time stood still.

It was like everyone stopped breathin', except Irma's and her whinin' was startin' to get on his nerves.

"Irma. Go on now."

There was a growl in his voice. The frustration was brewin', but I knew he wouldn't take it out on her.

"Daddy..." The tears clogged her throat, voice breakin' in between each syllable. "Please...let mama go..."

He growled in my ear, dropped his grip around my neck and kicked me as I hit the floor. Irma ran passed Black and grabbed me by the neck. The sadness on her face broke my heart, and the blood on her tiny hands from my neck frightened me. I knew this was no way for us to live, but I didn't have a plan. How was I gon take care of all these kids? I could flee to Birmingham, but then he'd kill us all and I didn't want no one sufferin' cause of me.

I was stuck.

I caught a glance of Black lookin' at Irma coddlin' me, afraid of her daddy. It was the first time I saw sorrow in his eyes. Thought for a second Irma seein' him would change his ways, but those emotions he felt was short-lived.

"I'll be back. Don't wait up."

He ran out the house and sped off, the dust kickin' up from the wheels. The boys ran from their room and helped me up and got somethin' to stop the bleedin'. Brenda came in the kitchen and finished the food, while Irma stayed in my arms on Black's chair. In that lil heart of hers she believed if she stayed in my lap, her daddy wouldn't come back and beat on me.

I admired her confidence.

For two weeks, Black came in and out of the house but never stayed the night.

I thought the boys would've left while he was gone, but they stayed a lil' longer and used that time to sneak food in the house. Wasn't much. They couldn't make it too obvious that there was more than what Black allowed us to have. Few eggs here and there, potatoes and carrots, onions, few herbs I ain't never heard of or cook with, two fresh cut chickens, some sweet cream butter and buttermilk. I ain't never used buttermilk before. They sell it at the market, but it cost more than regular milk, so I never bothered to try it.

The evenin' before the boys left, Black stayed home just to hump on me. He was so drunk, it wasn't 'bout five minutes and he was sleep.

In the mornin', the boys were up with their knapsacks off to the side. They usually take 'em to work, so it was nothin' different. I made sure I was up before Black, so I could get the biscuits ready. Made 'em with the buttermilk and added that sweet cream butter to it. I ain't never had nothin' melt in my mouth like dem biscuits.

Black shuffled into the kitchen and I had his

plate ready. He sat to the table and the boys ain't say not a word. The tension was thick, like he knew somethin' was different but couldn't place it.

"These biscuits taste different." He turned to me then back to the boys. "What you put in 'em?"

"Milk." I replied.

"You sassin' me?"

"No sir. Just answerin' what you ask me."

"I know you put somethin' different in these biscuits. You got some man givin' you food? These boys?"

Dennis shifted in his seat and Elijah held his hand to his arm to settle him down. "We're gonna head to work Ms. Roxie." Elijah grabbed everyone's plate and placed them in the sink. Charlie Jr. walked to me and kissed me on the cheek. "See you later mama." I smiled and handed him a large foil, it had extra biscuits for them. "For your lunch. You and the boys." He smiled back and headed to the door.

Black looked around confused. He just couldn't place what was happenin', so he drew the attention back on himself. "I'll be gone for two weeks. Sawmill got summa us working at a new plant out in Jackson."

"Since you gone so long, can I get extra money to have enough food for the kids?"

He smirked. "I'm feelin' good today, so here…" He reached in his pocket and pulled out a ten-dollar bill. "This nuff right here."

He gave this snicker, got up from the table then reach over to kiss me on the forehead. I inched back and he grabbed my neck, forcin' my face to his lips. Dennis got so angry he walked out and slammed the door. The slam caught Black's attention and he yell out after 'em.

"You boys short this week wit the money. Matter fact, ya'll been short the last two months. That man ain't payin' ya'll right?"

Charlie looked back at Black and turned to the door. "Nawh, he payin' us right." He looked back at me one mo' time, "Have a good day mama," then skipped down the steps.

Black looked back at me.

I turned to get the next set of food togetha for the younger ones and prepare them for school. I heard Black's feet shuffle out the door, then the car pulled off. I stood to the sink and said a small prayer for the boys while I fought through the sadness. The boys were smart enough to go to Mr. Tulman's and leave from there. One wouldn't know what Black would try to pull, so you had to be ten steps ahead all the time.

◆ ◆ ◆

Black showed up at Mr. Tulman's farm.

The boys were preparin' the plows when he pulled up. He was pissed to see they'd actually gone to work. He was sure they were leavin' and wanted to catch them at the bus since he was headed that way. Just a glimpse of them on the bus and he would've shot up the whole station.

"You Mr. Tulman?" He walked up to the shed, his eyes fixed on Dennis.

Tulman stood there with his arms folded, a wad of tobacco in his mouth, wide brim hat over his eyes. "Who's lookin' to know?"

Black gave a slick grin. "Dem boys you got workin' for you. I'm their daddy."

"Oh?"

"Yeah." He took a few steps closer. "I need to

ask you 'bout they pay. Seems like they've been short last couple weeks. They help with bills, so dem being short come out to be a problem."

Mr. Tulman raised his eyebrow and replied back with the same slick grin. The boys behind him, ready to make a move if need be.

"Reckon we got two different stories sir." He spat out some excess tobacco and continued. "From what I've been told, the boys make they money then give it to they father. Don't see none of it. Says they father don't take too kindly to other men helpin' out 'round the house."

Black's eyes were red with rage. He couldn't confirm his suspicions and he ain't know a thing 'bout Mr. Tulman. The man was too calm, too sure of himself. Made 'em think befo' reactin' like he normally do.

"Fine then." He backed up and gave a stare to the boys. "Guess it's just some misunderstandin' wit the boys that we'll talk about later."

Mr. Tulman spat out more tobacco, his stare cuttin' right through Black's body. "Guess so." He smirked. "Anythings else I can do for ya sir? The boys gotta lot of plowin' to do today. Reckon they should get started. Get paid for the hours they work."

Black looked back at the boys one last time.

"Guess so."

They looked at him with the same stare, then they headed in the shed to get to workin'. Mr. Tulman tipped his hat to Black then headed towards the shed.

"Enjoy your day sir."

Black stood there while all four of them headed into the shed. In less than a minute, the plows and tractors were goin' and the boys were drivin' 'cross the land to ready the crops. Pissed that he couldn't prove his suspicions, he left then headed to work. About an hour after Black left the farm, Mr. Tulman paid the boys for a day's worth of work and took 'em down to Montgomery where they caught the bus to Florida. It was the last any of us heard from the boys for months.

Later that afternoon, Black showed up at the house.

"Where dem boys?"

"Not sure. Ain't seen 'em since they left this

mornin'."

"How you they mama and don't know where they at?" He sucked his teeth and stormed in the house.

"Just the other day you said I wasn't they mama."

"What you say Roxie!?" He yelled from the back room.

"Nothin' Black."

I sat there on the porch and listened to him tear up the house I just finished cleanin'. Somethin' I'd gotten used to by now. Black figured he could tear up the house to find the answers he already knew. He thought tearin' up the house made him feel better, but all it did was anger him more 'cause he never found what he was lookin' for.

Never.

"Dem boys ain't git back here yet?" He stormed back out again with a bag in his hand.

"No Black. I ain't seen the boys since this mornin', same as you."

Black reached over and mushed my head

toward the ground. "You know where they is…" He made his way down the steps and to the car. "You gone git nuff of lyin' to me woman. I'll deal with you when I git back."

I wasn't sure if I was more relieved that he was leavin' or that the boys managed to escape this misery without gettin' caught and without me gettin' beat.

I got up to go in the house to fix myself somethin' to eat when Black yelled out the car window callin' my name.

"And don't look for that ten dollars. I took it." He laughed. "Since you don't know where dem boys are, you don't need all that extra money. Eat what you got."

I sorta laughed to myself.

Of all the places he looked, he ain't even notice the icebox. For the first time ever, I had nuff food to last me till he got back. Even had an extra bottle of that buttermilk to make them biscuits. Ain't even really care the milk would be gone by the time he got back.

Chapter —Eight

A Light in the Crystal

Bout a couple months after the boys left, I got pregnant with my sixth child. In the years later, I had Eliza, Betsy, Pauline and Michael. The only good thing that came from havin' kids with Black, is that I raised 'em how I want. Black ain't never let the eldest kids go to school, but all mine did.

Marley, Angela, Brenda and Irma would help out in the afternoon and weekends at Mr. Tulman's farm. I made sure I held onto the money he gave 'em. Kept it in a small box underneath the floorboard in the kitchen. It was loose from one of the many nights Black took his drunken rage out on me. Under there in the small box is where I kept the money and the letters the eldest would send me. Never got one from Lily. Mostly Pinky and Charlie Jr. They the ones that took a liking to me most. Always had it in my heart to leave, I just never knew when that would be.

Black got worse as the years went on.

Ain't matter what I said or did, he'd beat me just for breathin'. The rumors 'round town about him fatherin' other children grew. Got to a point where we stopped goin' to church. Too many folks talkin' 'bout he slept with all the women there and maybe even the Pastor's wife.

Can't worship the Lord when folk too busy mumblin' 'bout what yo husband did to them with his private parts. Had enuff insanity at home, ain't need it in church.

Wouldn't even give dem kids lunch money.

Had to make sure they had somethin' packed. The chil'ren at school would tease my babies, sayin' they daddy was givin' them fifty cent for school and he'd give my kids only a nickel.

One day, Marley came home cryin', upset from being teased. I'd gotten so fed up with the stories and the lies, that I confronted him. Ain't care about gettin' beat, but I wasn't gon let him keep treatin' his kids like dirt.

"Black." I stood in the living area next to the chair, hopin' he'd face me. "You know these kids out here teasin' these babies 'cause you givin' them more money than yo own."

He sat in his chair sippin' on that fancy beer like he always do, starin' into space with that expression. You could never tell if he was about to react or ignore you.

Neither were good.

He got up and stood straight for what felt like minutes, then took a long gulp of his beer and finished it off. The bottle in one hand, the other in his pant pocket. Fingers fiddlin' around with the change. He pulled his hand out and looked down, rubbin' his thumbs across the coins, countin' what he had and separatin' what he wanted to keep. He raised his eyes up at me, walked toward the kitchen table, stopped and cut his eyes, then dropped about a dollar in nickels and dimes on the table with the empty bottle, then left.

I never knew where he went for all those

hours, but I was certain other womens were involved. The days he did come home, he'd smell like some perfume, tobacco and whisky. A musk that women leave on a man when he's been with her.

Markin' their territory.

If I even had a thought of another man, Black would hear the thought and beat me for it. And trust, my love for him dwindled wit each hand that struck me. Made me feel like no other man would want me. Wit all these kids I kept havin', I was convinced no man would. Being unwanted added to the list of reasons why I ain't leave.

When Black was at work, Ms. Ann would come by and help with the kids and sneak a lil food in the house. I'd use it for lunch cause if Black knew he'd beat me.

There was a time in my marriage where the load got lighter. Only happened once a year, but during that time, it was like Heaven had truly came down to Earth.

Aunt Barb.

When she would visit, those were the best times. She was one of my favorites of my grandfather's kids, and whew Lawd was that woman feisty! Some folk say her and my mama were one in the same. I like to believe they were. Parts of me felt like if my mama was 'round, it woulda avoided me gettin' in this mess, but the Lord always reveals the reasons why things happen the way they do.

Aunt Barb lived in Birmingham, not too far from Cousin Sarah. She'd send clothes for the babies and a lil bit a cash I'd save up in the box with the other money. For maybe 'bout a year, I got away wit Black not noticin' the kids' clothes was lookin' nicer than they usually be. Finally, Black skipped work and set out to figure out how I was sneakin' in all this nice stuff. I ain't realized he ain't left, 'cause I only slept in the bed when he wanted to hump on me. Any other time, I'd take one of the old bunk bed mattresses from out back and put a sheet on it, so I'd have a lil comfort in the living room. With them being out back, I was bound to catch a bite from some bugs or whatever else crawled on it. Ain't had nothin' to clean it with properly.

That day, he stood over me like he was finna piss on me, holdin' up Michael's clothes askin' me where I got 'em from. I ain't wanna tell 'em it was from Aunt Barb. He'd heard 'bout her, but they ain't never met, so he'd think I was takin' up for some man, most likely Mr. Shepard. Not sure when he figure I had time to hump on another man, let alone talk to anybody.

"Still claimin' Aunt Barb bought these here clothes, huh?"

"Black it's too early to be fussin'. Ain't you got work?"

"I'm off today. And I'm gon get down to the bottom of who is sending these clothes."

"Black. It's too early for this. I gotta get the kids ready."

"Well, you go on. I'll be right here waitin' for 'Aunt Barb.'"

It just aggravated me more that I couldn't find no peace with Black. Him at work was the only time I had quiet. I ain't do much, ain't had no friends, hardly went into town 'cause I ain't had no money, so him 'round durin' the day, took away the lil' peace I could get.

Ms. Ann came by and I had to shoo her off before Black saw her. I sat on the porch so I could catch her. Mr. Shepard waved hello but I just looked the other way and caught a glimpse Black lookin' out the window. He was a miserable man who refused to allow others to be happy. He had to infect his own personal misery on others. Lil did he know, a temporary fix for that misery was soon to show up unexpected.

After I made sure Mr. Shepard and Ms. Ann knew Black was 'round, I got the kids ready for school and started breakfast. I'd get Marley to sneak over that buttermilk from Mr. Tulman's, so we'd at least have somethin' nice to eat among all the mess Black put us through. It reminded me of the boys. Whatever would keep me goin', I took it.

I hated when Black was around.

I could feel him puttin' that energy out there that I was wrong and he was gearin' up to give me a whoppin' the likes I ain't never seen for lyin'. It was tense in the house. Alls I wanted to do is get the kids out before anythin' bad happened. Marley, Brenda, Angela and Irma were out the door to school. Eliza, Betsy and Pauline were in the room playin', and I had sat to the table to feed me and Michael, when a horn from outside blew.

I ain't ever seen Black move that fast.

He ran to that door and watched the car park in front of the house. It was a light blue 1954 Buick. Back then ain't too many womens drove cars, so it was always a sight to see when one did. Out the door, in this navy blue skirt with a white fancy sweater, these polka dot shoes, navy gloves and some kinda brooch in her hair, my Aunt Barb sashayed out that car with her bag in hand.

"And you must be Black." She looked at him, the house, then him again. "I assume my niece is inside."

Black stood at the top step lookin' like he was 'bout to pee his pants. I ain't ever seen Black shook over no woman. Can't recall no woman I met that was like Aunt Barb. Her skin was so smooth it looked like chocolate. She wore this press powder on her face that made it shine, had this sparkle on it. Always kept her hair pressed and in a French roll. And she knew how to step in dem heels. That sassy walk would tear down a room and she knew how to command 'tention.

I waited to see if Black was gonna say somethin' slick like he always do, but he just stood there. Figured he was so shocked he was wrong, he ain't know how to respond.

"You just gon stand there, or you gon come get these bags, so I can see about my niece?" She looked at him with a side glare. Waitin' for 'em to say somethin'. I had a mind that Aunt Barb woulda backhanded him like he was her child.

Black moved so fast down them steps.

"And there's two more in the back seat if you don't mind, sir."

"No ma'am." His head looked down to the ground. "I'll grab those too."

I had to laugh.

Aunt Barb would come by to see me right before the kids got outta school and she'd stay the whole summer. Did that for years.

Black would be sure to stay out.

He ain't want no parts of Aunt Barb and she ain't play dat puttin' hands on a woman mess. Black tried it one time and Aunt Barb headed towards that shotgun and was ready to take him out. That day, I wish she would've, but I know she ain't want no jail time.

I respected that.

Life Ain't Been No Crystal Stair

From that point on, Black steered clear of Aunt Barb.

When she was around, we ate good, went out into town and went shoppin'. She'd help me with the babies and get 'em goin'. I let 'em play outside whiles we talk and did women's stuff. I ain't never had my nails painted, but Aunt Barb would paint my nails and press my hair so I wouldn't look so old and used.

Black would run in and out to get a change of clothes. For those quick moments, he wouldn't even be drunk. He'd say "yes ma'am" and "no ma'am" to Aunt Barb.

Those were the best summers I ever had.

Every time she left, you'd think it was somebody's funeral. I would cry and carry on for days. I knew the moment she left, everythin' would start up agin. Black would see me cryin' upset that Aunt Barb had to go and throw his shoe at me. Tell me to hush up that noise.

I wish I had the courage to stand up to him the way Aunt Barb did. I wish I had the conviction to just grab the gun, or stick somethin' in his food and kill 'em, but the Lord ain't make me that way.

I'd be depressed for days once she was gone. It was back to the same ol' routine of him humpin' and beatin' on me. Oftentimes, I wondered what type of example I was settin' for my girls and my boy. Ain't want them to think this how a marriage was 'posed to be. Ain't want my son thinkin' it was right to hit on a woman, and I damn sure ain't want my girls to believe gettin' beat was some type of love and that they had to sit there and take.

They didn't.

They ain't have a strong enough mama to get out, at least, that's what I let Black convince me to believe. It would take me awhile, many years in fact, but I found I wasn't no different than Aunt Barb. I just had to find it in myself to believe it.

Chapter Nine

Dirty Glass

It was the 60's. By that time, Marley, Angela, Brenda and Irma followed the rest of their siblings and left to Florida. My girls were growin' up and movin' out. Angela was always the strong one and she told me she'd get me out this hell hole one day. Pinky and I were pretty close. She sent word that I could come and stay with her and the family. Always knew eventually the kids would be my savin' grace. I just had to find the right time.

The girls wrote me letters and sent money. I know they hoped it would convince me to leave, but I'd just save in the box underneath the floorboard along wit the rest.

I loved gettin' letters in the mail. Made me feel good to read what the kids wrote and they'd always sent pictures.

Orlando was beautiful.

They had all different types of trees and the air just looked clean. It was nice and built up there. Wasn't all country like Camp Hill. I was happy to see pictures of the beach. Ain't never been to one and wondered what it felt like to have the sand in my toes. All of it seemed like a dream that would never come true, so I lived through the pictures.

I'd catch myself starin' in space thinkin' 'bout Orlando, and Black would always kill my daydream, askin' what I'm starin' into space for; like he needed me to be lookin at him so I could listen to 'em fuss all day. He was so caught up in himself, he actually thought peoples like to hear him talk. We all just wanted him to go somewhere else and be quiet for a change.

And he was actin' more and more crazy.

Heard he was out in the streets more drunk than he usually be. Was no win wit 'em. Wasn't ever gonna change.

Ain't seen somebody so confused 'bout what was happenin' in they own home. Couldn't understand why his kids was leavin'. He truly believed he was a good father and provider, despite the fact he ain't never done nothin' for the dem kids or me.

He was livin' in a fairytale.

But it wasn't like mine was his only kids.

He thought I ain't know he had kids out there, but I knew. Had kids all over the place, enough to start a new family many times over. I often wish he'd just go stay with all those women he gave chil'ren to, but he'd always come back to me. Made it seem like I should feel special 'bout it. Really, I wish I was one of those women he dropped his seed in and left. They ain't have to deal wit 'em beatin' on 'nem like he did me. There was no reason why I'd feel special at all.

All that was left was Eliza, Betsy, Pauline, Michael, and Edie.

It was the first time I ain't have a whole bunch of chil'ren in the house. I was 'fraid Black would be 'round more.

Few years later, Alaine, Myra and Larry showed up. By then, the eldest in the house were in middle school and I was back to raisin' babies all over. I was forty-two when I had Larry. He was my last. I was tired of havin' kids. Even went to a doctor who was 'pose to prescribe me somethin' to stop it. Don't know if it worked but I was lucky no mo' came after him.

Black was old, almost sixty, but he still moved around town like he was thirty-five. Womens would walk pass the house and see me outside with the kids playin' and cut they eyes at me. I knew they had to be messin' wit Black. He probably thought he was doin' right by not bringin' it in the home, but I don't think those women were brave enough to come in here. If they did, they'd probably stop messin' wit 'em and then I'd just get beat for scarin' off his women.

His brothers and 'nem would still stop by the house. Black was the oldest boy out of dem all. I knew some of them treated their wives bad so it kinda made sense where it all came from. Ain't expect too much help from his family, even though they was nice to me and the kids. Back then, nobody wanted to get in peoples business, so they kept quiet. Let it go on as if it didn't exist, but it did.

Life Ain't Been No Crystal Stair

My peace of mind was always short-lived when it came to Black.

Every night, he got worse.

He'd come in so drunk, he ain't had no idea who's house he was in or what woman he thought he saw. And each time, he'd push himself on me, moanin' and groanin', breath smellin' like whisky and old tobacco, skin clammy from the outside, his scent like a horse mixed with some random women's perfume. For days, it was the same: work, dinner, out in the street, drunk sex with me. Ain't hardly healed from Larry comin' outta me and his musty body was all on me.

This was my life — rinse and repeat.

In the Fall of '69, I got a letter from Marley and Angela sayin' they were comin' to visit wit they husbands for the holiday, and that made me happy. Wish I was able to see them get married, be there, help 'em get dressed, do more than what my family did for me, but I couldn't.

Each time Black would leave money in the house, I'd take it and get new linens to prepare for their arrival. I'd see Mr. Shepard on my travels and he'd always offer me a ride downtown. He hated that I walked 'round town with all the kids by myself, but I ain't mind it. The walk downtown always gave me time to think. My thoughts would be the same, how to get me and the kids away from Black's crazy behind.

That year, we had Thanksgiving at Ms. Beulah's. It was the first time in years since we spent a holiday with other people. Ms. Beulah made the turkey and since everybody liked my greens, I made those. It was almost a treat when Black would bring some collards in, which was rare just like everythin' else. Along wit the collards, I made yams, and a small pot of rutabaga for Pauline. I don't know who got her to eatin' some rutabaga, but she'd always ask for it the few times we'd get to have dinner with Ms. Beulah.

Ms. Ann's help me put togetha a pecan pie. Used some of that bourbon Black had lyin' 'round. He had so much of it, I'm sure he ain't miss it. When I put it on the table, he looked at me tryin' to figure out how I got the stuff to make it. Wasn't no way I was gonna tell on Ms. Ann. Ms. Beulah lied and said she brought the stuff over while he was at work so

I could make it. He still looked at me with a bit of suspicion but he let it go.

That don't happen too many times.

Had some clothes Aunt Barb sent. Her stuff was so nice, that I liked to hold onto it for when I needed it most. All the girls were 'bout the same size at the same ages, so it always worked in my favor,' specially since Black never gave me money to buy clothes. If the clothes ain't come from Aunt Barb I made them.

Ms. Beulah had the Pastor over for dinner with his family and we all sat to the table and ate. First time I ever felt at peace at a kitchen table, not worried 'bout whether Black was gon' toss the food 'cross the room over somethin' that meant nothin'. I smiled listenin' to everyone's talk. The kids were happy, there was no fussin', no cussin', just a family enjoyin' each other. I took it all in as much I could, 'cause I ain't know how the night would end.

A few hours later, we left and went home. I'm sure Black went to some other woman's house, 'cause the next mornin' the bed was empty. I'd wondered how I slept so good, then I saw he wasn't there. He must've enjoyed himself 'cause he stayed out the house. I tried not to get used to the quiet too much.

"Mama, why daddy ain't never here in the mornin'?" Betsy came and stood next to me while I made breakfast.

"Yo daddy like to stay out and hang wit his friends baby." I continued scramblin' the eggs, then put them off to the side and began fixin' the potatoes.

"How come we don't meet none of his friends?"

I glanced over my shoulder. "You really wanna meet yo daddy's friends?"

She smiled. "Not really." I chuckled. "That's what I thought."

"You puttin' onions in the potatoes?"

"Is that how you wan 'em?"

"Well, since daddy ain't here and he don't like onions —"

"Or peppers," I cut in.

"Can you add 'em?"

I looked over and smiled at her. The kids loved Black, but they were a lot more loyal to me.

"Sure baby."

I planted a kiss on her forehead, then reached in the cupboard for the onions and peppers. Seem like God was on my side that day 'cause I ain't see Black 'til it was almost time for the kids to go to bed. He came in and took a bath, changed his clothes, put a few dollars on the dresser and left again.

That woman he wit must cook good too.

Christmas was a few days away and I decided to decorate the house. I spent more than twenty Christmas holidays in here and ain't never decorated the house. Figured since Marley and Angela were comin' to surprise me, I'd fix up the house as much I could. Still hadn't told Black they were comin', hopin' it'd be a nice surprise.

And quite the surprise it was.

While Black was at work Mr. Shepard showed me how to put up the lights, so I did that and added some garland around the porch, along with a few of those big red bows. It wasn't much but I felt it was nice.

Christmas Eve came around and the girls showed up early wit they husbands. Had to give it to 'em, those were some nice lookin' mens they found, had manners too. Felt bad we still live in this shack, but they ain't judge. I'm sure the girls told 'em how they grew up.

I was excited 'cause it'd be the first time in a long time that the girls was home and my youngest kids was so excited to see 'em. I was able to get a few cornish hens from the market with the money that Black gave me and added some herbs to it. I spent a lot of time with Ms. Ann while the kids were in school, so I watched her cook a lot. Paid 'tention to how she'd season her meats and vegetables. I was able to make squirrel and coon taste just like chicken.

Mostly everybody was eatin' by the time Black got in the house.

Drunk as usual.

"Who the hell all these people?" He stumbled about across the livin' room floor. I saw the anger in his eyes 'cause there were men sittin' 'round the table.

"Roxie? Who the hell all these people?"

"Yo kids Black. You don't recognize Marley and Angela?"

"Who's all these mens in here?"

"This man right here," I pointed to my left, "is Angela's husband Leonard. And this one right here is Marley's husband Sam."

"So yo ass let 'em leave, then come back in here wit husbands?" He walked over to the kitchen and I saw both Sam and Leonard shift sides in the chair to block both Angela and Marley. "When the hell they get married?" He yelled. "See, they ain't give two shits about you. Got married and ain't even tell you. And yous helping 'em leave the house. What you got to say 'bout yaself, goin' 'gainst me."

"I knew they were married Black."

Marley looked over at me and shook her head for me to keep quiet.

"Yo ass knew they were married and ain't tell me..." He looked at me, chest heavin', hate in his eyes, sweaty from outside and whatever other smell comin' from his skin.

"Wasn't my place to tell."

"Ma!" Marley yelled.

She looked at me again, knowin' Black would beat me for sassin' him. Thing is, I wasn't sassin' him or even tryin', it's just what came out my mouth.

"Oh…" His steps got closer, then Sam stood so close in front of me I thought he was gon sit in my lap. "So you think, it wasn't yo place to tell me they was comin' to my house?"

"Black, come on now. We have people here."

"These ain't no people, these my kids. They ain't no guest in this house that I paid for. I keep these lights on, this water runnin', this food on the table and all you got to do is right by me and you can't even do that!"

"Black, maybe you should —"

"Maybe, I should whoop yo ass!"

He reached over Sam and slapped me so hard I hit the floor, then walked over by the side of the sink and started throwin' all the food off the counter, knockin' everything to the ground in a rage. Black grabbed that shotgun, cocked it and shot a bullet through the roof. Made sure no one got brave. I was only a few feet from 'em. He grabbed me by my hair and dragged me 'cross the floor.

It happened so fast.

Leonard and Sam tried to grab me from Black's grip but it was like he had the strength of ten men. Everybody in the neighborhood heard me. And it ain't like they ain't never heard me before. Guess this time they all got tired of it and made their way outside. Mr. Shepard was the first to show up.

The guys tussled with Black tryna to hold him back from me, loosen his grip on my hair and keep clear of that shotgun cause his hands were on the trigger. Was only the Lord who prevented that thing from goin' off and killin' somebody. With all that tusslin', somehow, Black spotted Mr. Shepard behind me tryin' pull me out from under him. That ain't do nothin' but make things worse 'cause soon as Black got a clear eye of 'em, he lost what bit of sense he had left.

"So you sleepin' wit my wife Shep! Huh? You sleepin' wit my wife?"

"Black, you know I ain't sleepin' with Roxie."

"What you over there for, huh? Move then, lemme handle this wit my wife."

Sam and Leonard pulled him back before he could reach for me again, but his anger was too much and he broke free, snatched me by my neck pounded my face in. I screamed for Black to stop but he ain't care. It took Marley and Angela's husbands, along with Mr. Shepard to pull him off me. The girls ran to pull me out of harm's way but the damage I had already been done.

Ms. Ann called the police.

Once they got there, he tried to blame it all on Mr. Shepard, claimin' he was bringin' order to his house, that Mr. Shepard was sleepin' wit me. As much as Black cheated I ain't never put up a fuss. He was convinced, in his own mind, that it was OK to sleep wit other women and expect me to sleep wit him too and have all his babies. He was convinced that wouldn't no other man be interested in me outside of him and that I wasn't worthy of being done right by a man. Black couldn't 'splain right why he did what he did.

And the police wasn't 'bout to let go any of it.

Black was arrested and shoved in the back of that car. I did my best not to feel no shame, but I couldn't help but feel like I could've changed all this if I had the strength to leave.

Most folk say it's easier to stay when your husband, or any man, beats on you and that may be so, but what I learned is that it's not 'bout stayin', so much as it is dyin'. Although Black beat on me, I'd never let him kill me. I stayed alive and let my faith in the Lord, as well as the hope that I'd at least be able to do better by my youngest, keep me livin', despite livin' in hell.

I ain't let Black steal my joy.

I found peace wherever I could, even in the smallest of things and that's what angered Black the most — that he couldn't break me. No matter how hard he tried, he couldn't break me.

That night Angela told me enough is enough, I was going back with them to Florida. I packed my clothes, grabbed that money from the floorboard, and got me and the kids bus tickets. Larry, Myra, Alaine and Edie went with me while Eliza, Betsy, Pauline and Michael, stayed with Ms. Beulah 'till we could go back and get 'em. Angela called over Black's job to made sure his boss ain't bail him out.

In two weeks, all us was outta that house.

Lord knows I ain't think it could happen, but just like that, we was all, outta that daggone house.

Finally, I was free.

Chapter Ten

Translucent

Orlando was more than I could imagine from those pictures the kids sent me. It was beautiful.

Nothin' like I ever seen, and I ain't seen much. First thing I wanted to do, I had to do, was walk on that beach. I'd seen it so many times in the postcards, had to experience it for myself. Ain't never seen water so blue. The sound of the waves crashin' had to be one of the most peaceful sounds I ever heard. It was more confirmation that God is real.

I took my shoes off and let the soles of my feet

grip the sand. It felt like grain. Like a smooth and rough feelin' I couldn't really describe. Somethin' like cardboard but soft like powder. There was a crisp taste in the air. Smelled so good. Even how the wind swayed the trees was different. I heard about the ocean, seen pictures of it in school, but there's nothin' like puttin' yo hands in it.

Touchin' it.

It was a far cry from the wells back in Camp Hill.

I caught up with Pinky. She was so happy to see me. I'd grown closer to her, but Lily was still distant from me. She got married and moved to Arkansas, while Sarah moved up North.

I ain't blame her none.

She made sure to move far away. I'm certain it's 'cause she wanted to create a new life for herself. Of all the kids, she suffered the most. I'd think about her often, lay awake at night wishin' I was brave enough to run in the room and save her from that monster she called daddy.

I've killed Black many times in my head over the years.

There's times I'd watch him sleep, look at the gun rack over the bed, want to pull the trigger and blow his head off. Just didn't have it in me. I couldn't save her or myself at that time.

Once I got settled, Pinky allowed me and the kids to stay with her and helped me get on welfare. Soon enough, I was able to get my own apartment. Ain't even bother me that it was small. It was a sight for sore eyes compared to that two-bedroom shack I lived since I was eighteen.

We was able to get good and sturdy furniture, not the raggedy frail mess Black had us sleepin' and sittin' on. Brenda helped me decorate the house, while Irma helped with the laundromat a few times before I got it down. I was still usin' a washboard to keep the kids' clothes clean. They were all still small, so it was easy enough. Habits are hard to break, plus I didn't mind.

The kids had clean sheets, decent mattresses, pillows with feathers in 'em and air condition. Things that were normal to most people, but a luxury for us. And our neighborhood was so nice. Everythin' was in walking distance. There was a mix of city and country, but even the country wasn't all that country. There were so many stores to choose from.

And grocery shoppin'…

Lord knows I ain't no what to do! Gettin' those food stamps gave me so many options. When you been killin' coon and squirrel most ya life, makin' stew from scraps, and whatever else you can eat from, government cheese is like eatin' steak.

We ate good.

The kids ain't even know I could cook good I as did.

Since I ain't have no real job yet, the kids gave me money here and there to watch the grandbabies. Even got me a TV. I ain't never watch no TV before, and to see it in color was somethin' else. I heard shows used to be in black and white, but since we ain't never have no TV I ain't really know the difference. There was so much to watch. Some days, I'd be up for hours watchin' TV 'till it cut off after midnight.

It was the first time in my life I felt truly happy.

I would meet people at the grocery store and neighbors around the apartment. I never really knew how to talk to people until I moved to Florida. The only people that talked to me back home was my chil'ren, along with Ms. Ann and Mr. Shepard.

Life Ain't Been No Crystal Stair

When Black's brothers would stop to the house, I got close wit Millie. She was married to one of his brothers. Outside Ms. Ann, she was the most grown up company I had.

My youngest were in school and doin' good. On weekends, we'd go uptown or play at the park. On Sunday's, we'd all scrunch up in my apartment and have Sunday dinner. Even found me a good church home where I could attend service. I thought about gettin' my license and learnin' how to drive. I know my oldest kids ain't mind takin' me 'round town, but somethin' in me wanted to finally do for myself 'cause Black ain't never care to teach me. Prolly thought I'd pack the kids up on one of his drunk nights and leave.

I enjoyed being 'round all my grandbabies. Every mother always look forward to seein' her chil'ren wit chil'ren. It's a line you begin the first time you have a baby. You see yo young, have young of they own and you look 'round at what you created proud and happy. By the time I'd moved to Orlando, I had 'quite a few grandkids. Some of them was few years older than my own.

I was amazed at the family I had waitin' for me all this time here.

I knew life could be this good, but to see how it felt firsthand was nothin' short of amazin'. I thought of Grandpa often. How he'd feel seein' all his grandkids, great-grands and great-great grands, and me being in some ways, on my own two feet. I reckon he'd be mighty proud.

I thought of Uncle Willie and Aunt Martha, just as much.

Was able to send a postcard to Cousin Sarah and Aunt Barb to let them know I moved. Just when I was startin' to believe I was ready to move on, Black showed up.

Don't even know how he found me.

Wondered if I'd left one of the postcards with the address of the kids there and somehow he found it. He loved to tear up the house when things ain't go his way, so I'm almost certain of it.

It been six months since we left Camp Hill and every other week, I'd get calls or letters beggin' me to come back. I just ignored it. The kids was almost outta school for the year. Summer break was 'bout to begin, and as I got ready to head down the street to do laundry. I opened the door and Black was on the other side. I had a mind to scream, and I should've but I didn't.

He stood at my front door, beggin' me to come back.

No was on my tongue, but never reached my lips.

"I miss you Roxie." Black got down on his knees, hands clasped together as if he were praying to God for Him to hear him. "Look, I know I was wrong. Gimme one 'mo chance. I can do betta. Just come home Roxie, please."

No.

"Black, I don't know if I can trust yo word."

"Roxie please. I done wrong. I'm sorry. Just please, you and the kids come back." He continued to beg. "I'll change. I promise. We can go to church together, I'll stop drinkin', I just want my family."

No.

"We doin' real good here and I don't wanna mess this up for the kids."

He looked up at me and the sorry lookin' face quickly turned back to the mean one I knew best.

"We ain't live good?"

"Black, if you got to ask then I'm not sure what to tell you."

"Roxie, please!"

"Black, I don't want no trouble wit you. I got to go do laundry." I made my way down the steps. He was still on his knees. I knew for certain if he even reached to hit me, there was no way I would even think about it. "You should go."

His eyes followed me down the steps. "Is you gon at least think on it?"

"I'll think 'bout it." I looked back at him still on the steps, then made my way down the street to the laundry.

When I got back, Dennis and Charlie, Jr. was on the steps waitin' for me. I knew Black got hold to a few of his kids. Try to get them sway my decision his way. Ain't never knew a man to believe such fairy tales about they life as Black did. None of his kids cared for him.

None.

I saw it all on they faces.

It spoke the words that didn't need to be said. They knew my heart still loved Black and would go back just to see for myself if things would change. They knew me. Still, they took the time to plead they case in me not leavin' 'cause they cared that much. 'Specially Charlie Jr. He took a likin' to me most.

Dennis looked at me already exhausted, knowin' the back and forth that was 'bout to happen. "Ms. Roxie, please tell me you ain't goin' back."

I stood to the steps waitin' for them to let me through. "I don't know."

"Awh c'mon mama, you know." CJ sighed. He grabbed the laundry cart from me so I could open the door. When I walked in, almost all the kids were there waitin' on me. Word quickly got 'round they daddy had come to bring me back to Camp Hill and it was like a courtroom in that apartment.

The younger kids was in they room playin'. In between the living room and the kitchen was Marley, Angela, Brenda, Pinky, Elijah, and Irma. I felt like I was on trial for even thinkin' twice 'bout goin' back. I couldn't deny I felt a bit sorry for 'em and believed that maybe he did change. That maybe me leavin' was the fire he needed to get his tail to get right. I believed it so much, I tried to plead this with my kids.

Of course they ain't buy not one bit of it.

Pinky practically begged me not to go, but told me not to give up on my food stamps or my apartment if I did.

"You know how daddy is" she said.

We all knew Black was quick to get mad and not to be trusted. Despite me havin' just a lil' faith that he'd changed, we all knew, even me, that it'd be a matter of time before Black went back to his ways. Somethin' he couldn't quite let go of even if he tried. But then again, I ain't sure if he really tried at all.

It was 'bout three days since Black showed up on my doorstep. Same as the three days I waited when he first proposed. On that third day, I packed up my stuff and the kids and went back to Camp Hill. We'd been gone over six months and here we was, walkin' back into the mess I worked hard to get us out of.

Irma and Brenda moved into my apartment to keep it up, just in case. I ain't tell Black bout me being on welfare, and as long as I didn't let them folks know otherwise, they kept sendin' the money to the house. As if nothin' was different, as if I'd never left.

But I did.

Black was too happy on that road back. I felt the hurt from my kids. I knew I'd done them wrong, just when I'd finally done 'em right. We was all quiet on the way back. Black tried to hold onto my hand, but I barely held onto his. He knew I ain't wanna go, but that hold he had on me was strong. Now that I think 'bout it, I'm sure the thought of Black constantly showin' up to the house 'till I finally gave in was cause for me to just go. I ain't want a second helpin' of Camp Hill all the way in Orlando.

Few hours later, we pulled up onto that dusty road, the house lookin' like the same mess we left six months ago. I caught a glimpse of Ms. Ann in her window as we passed by and I saw the disappointment. She hoped to God I was strong enough to resist him. I know she prayed for the strength I needed, but just like I wasn't ready to leave Camp Hill for Orlando, I wasn't ready to be strong the way I needed to be, not yet.

Thing is…

Her prayers were 'bout to be answered a lot sooner than both us thought.

Chapter Eleven

Broken Glass

The summer of 1970 wasn't as fun as I hoped it to be. I started out in Florida having fun in the sun with my kids and enjoyin' life for the first time. Now, I done brought us ten, twenty steps back. Despite how I felt, Black seem like he changed.

There was food in the house.

Not as much food as I had back at the apartment, but a lot more food than we ever had livin' there. The rooms were still the same, Larry stayed in the room with me and Black, while the other six shared that one large room with three separate beds.

Life Ain't Been No Crystal Stair

Kids wasn't too happy. They ain't play much.

My hands were full with Larry when Ms. Ann stopped by to sit with me. I knew she wanted to ask me why I came back, I'm sure everyone wanted to ask me why I came back, but I said 'till death do us part. If things just ain't work out 'tween me and Black, he could never say I ain't try. He could never go before God and say I left him without 'cause, that he made an effort to make our marriage work and I just gave up on 'em. He could never say that, no matter how much he would want to, he could never say I gave up on 'em.

Black took us all to the movies one evenin', and made me think that maybe he did change. Paid for everythin', no fuss. Bought us all popcorn and sodas to share. Even walked 'round town for a bit before headin' back home. I made dinner, he ate it with no fuss and in that moment, I was glad I made the decision to give things one mo' try.

Two weeks later, Black came home drunk.

I ain't wanna assume nothin', so I kept the kids out his way while he sat and let the liquor pass through.

Next mornin', he was passed out on that chair.

That same sweaty, musty scent. I was nervous that ol' nice Black was short-lived, but again, I ain't wanna assume nothin' so I made breakfast as usual, then got the kids ready for church. I reached for Black to let 'em know we was goin' to service when he grabbed my hand and began to twist my arm. In my mind I was tryna figure out where that came from cause I ain't do nothin' to cause him to react that way to me, then I remember...this Black. I ain't never had to do nothin' for 'em to put his hands on me.

Most times nothin' was just enough reason.

"Why you got yo hand on me woman?" He continued to twist my arm under me, his eyes large, bulgin' at me. I looked over and saw the kids run back in the room, except Michael. He stood there. His eyes fixed on Black's hand and mine. "You tryna smack me woman?"

"Black, alls I was comin' to do was tell you me and the kids goin' to service, that's all. You ain't gotta twist my arm."

"Oh! You think 'cause you was out there in Florida, you can just do what you want?"

Black raised his hand and slapped me to the ground. Larry was still in my arms. Michael ran over to me, grabbed Larry and gave Black the hardest stare. I thought he had a mind to hit Michael, but he looked back at 'em, then at me and slapped me again. I shook my head at Michael not to go up 'gainst Black. I saw it in his eyes that he wanted to. He was only in the fourth grade, but he had anger in his eyes that day. Wasn't no need for me and him to get beat, 'cause believe me, we both woulda got beat.

We never made it to church that day.

What I ran away from it came right back, and it didn't take much for it to happen again. We'd barely been back a few weeks and he was back to his old self. Drinkin', out all times of the night, yellin', tossin' food all over the place, dirtyin' up the house after I spent all day cleanin' it, slappin' me all up and down the house. Black was older so he couldn't move as fast as he used to, but that heavy hand ain't change. Seems he got stronger since I'd left or maybe the liquor in 'em made it seem like he was stronger.

Still, he beat on me.

All that beggin' and pleadin' was nothin' but a fairy tale. I was so glad I ain't let nothin' I had back in Orlando go. I was mad for being so stupid, but I ain't have time to fuss at myself. I knew I had to leave again. I was just waiting for my moment.

While the kids were out playin' and Black was gone, I checked all the loose floorboards and the cupboards to see if Black was hidin any money 'round the house for whatever reason. I gathered up any extra money I could find since the kids would take turns sendin' me money. Made sure I got the mail before he came home. I'd keep it hidden in the box under the floorboard. In a couple of weeks, I had enough to leave with me and the kids, but I wanted enough to hold me over once I got to Florida. I had a mind to get me a job once I left. Make sure I had no reason to come back.

As the days passed Black got bold with his affairs.

The women would come 'round lookin' for Black, starin' me down, hopin' I'd say somethin' so they could go back to him, knownin' he'd beat on me just for defendin' myself. I never said anythin' to 'em. Just let 'em talk and walk pass. They knew Black was at work, just testin' me to see how far I'd go.

Got so bad, when I saw 'em comin' down the road, me and the kids would go back in the house and close the door 'till they walk on pass.

Life Ain't Been No Crystal Stair

Thought that would keep me outta harm's way, but that seemed to piss Black off more. I'll never understand how one person could be so mean and spiteful to someone who did everythin' for 'em. I ain't never done Black wrong, but every day from the time we was married, 'till I left, Black did me and all his kids so dirty. Filthy dirty.

I'll never understand it.

And me speakin' back with Mr. Shepard ain't help not one bit. Seem like Black would come home early on purpose just to try and catch me in somethin' that ain't never happen. One afternoon he called himself comin' home from lunch. I barely smiled at Mr. Shepard and Black ran up on the porch so fast, dragged me down by my neck and beat me in the middle of the livin' room.

I always feared for my life 'round Black, and each day I thought could be my last. The pattern continued: work, get drunk, leave the house, come back at the crack of dawn, bathe, eat, leave. Rinse and repeat. In between there, he'd find time to beat on me and they wasn't like befo', they got worse each time.

They started a midday prayer at church and I took the kids one Wednesday afternoon. While in service, I prayed for God to let me know when it was the right time to go. Sure, I know what you thinkin', ANYTIME was the right time, but honestly, there was too much at stake this second time. Black had reached a new level of crazy and it's not that he wasn't crazy befo', but all those threats he used to make in the past ain't seem so empty no mo'. In my spirit, I knew he'd make good on those threats and still, I couldn't get no one caught up in the mess I made.

I had to be like my kids.

I had to put it in my mind that it was happenin' and do it. That's the only way. Either that or death and Lord knows I wasn't ready to die.

Later on that evenin', I had dinner fixed. Black ain't say much when he got home, which made me think I might be in the clear. He sat to the table, ate, and then left out like he usually do.

It had to be between two or three o'clock in the mornin'. I was sleep, in a deep sleep and was woke up so fast by my body bein' thrown in the air. Ain't have to catch my bearin'. My back hit the dresser and it felt like my lung collapsed. My chest bruisin' up real fast. I hadn't regained consciousness yet and Black was screamin' so. Couldn't pick up what he was sayin' cause my hearin' hadn't clear yet. Me not answerin' him got 'em even more mad and before I could try to respond, I was being dragged by my scalp out the room, down the hall and into the livin' room where he straddled me and pounded my face.

He just kept punchin'.

I never did respond to what he was askin' 'cause I couldn't gather myself to hear 'em right. But I ain't really need to know what he was askin'. I knew this was 'bout one of Black's women seein' Mr. Shepard speakin' to me at church. Even though I never said a word, even though I never entertained Mr. Shepard of all the years we lived in this house, just him callin' after me was enough reason for Black to assume I was cheatin' which, in his mind, gave him just cause to beat on me.

Of all of the beatin' I got from Black, this one was the worse. He beat me until he tired himself out and passed out on the floor from bein' so drunk and in a rage. The blood dripped from my face. Ain't have the strength to walk, so I crawled to the bathroom, pulled myself up to the sink, grabbed my washcloth and wiped my face. I had to be gentle. Just me hoverin' my hand over my face hurt. Wanted to fix me a bath so bad and soak my body but I just ain't have the strength.

I wobbled into the hall to check and see if Black was still out and he hadn't moved an inch. I turned right into the kids' room and they were still sleep, or at least pretended to be sleep.

I ain't even look.

I went in the closet, grabbed our bags and threw in all their clothes and shoes. I slid the floorboard back, grabbed the money, and put it in the side pocket of the bag so I'd remember not to leave it.

After I packed all the kids' clothes, I went back in the room where I slept and checked on Larry. He was still sleep. I ain't worry 'bout my stuff 'cause I ain't bring much. I laid across the foot of the bed and let my tears take me to sleep, which wasn't long.

The pain kept me in and out.

Woke up with Black still on the floor. I got his lunch ready for work and pushed 'em over a 'lil with my foot to wake 'em up. He grumbled, wrestled 'round, then sat straight up. I took a few herbs I had in the fridge and boiled me some tea. When he got up, I was sittin' to the table quiet.

Black was so hungover, he woke up like nothin'

happened the night before. I gave him his lunch and walked him to the door. I watched him get in the car and drive away. I waved 'cause I knew it'd be the last time he'd ever get a lunch or a wave from me. Black ain't never been right and was never gon change. I had to live or get ready to die and I chose to live.

The kids were up by that time.

Everyone got dressed, then I got myself togetha. I packed last minute things, put the money from the side pocket in my purse and walked out the front door. Ain't even look back this time. I just kept walkin' as fast I could. It ain't matta how heavy Larry got on my arm, the kids and I kept walkin'.

Nearin' the main road to the bus station, I ran into Deacon Johnson from the church. He saw my face, the bags, the kids and immediately stopped. He ain't say a word, he knew what to do. We all packed in Deacon Johnson's car and he took us to the station. As I walked through the plaza, I ran into Ms. Beulah and Black's brother Howard.

I froze.

I was scared to death they would get a hold to Black and he'd come drag me and the kids from the station. Ms. Beulah walked over to me, saw my face and smiled.

"If he ain't gone act right then just leave. You deserve better Roxie."

His brother ain't put up no fuss, so I figured he agreed. She kissed the kids and we hurried along. I got all us bus tickets, called down to Charlie Jr. and in about eight hours, I was back in Orlando.

Camp Hill would never be my home again.

I heard somebody say once, only you know when you've had enough. Even though I thought I had enough wit Black, it wasn't the final straw. Me knowin' for certain there was no way that man would change his ways was enough. Call me forgivin', naive, or whatever you want, but I believe God has a way of changin' people who want to be changed. I believe that if a person feels they've had a enough of doin' wrong, God will make a way for them to get back on His path. He did it with David, Saul, Mary Magdalene and a bunch of other folks. If those folk can go from being bad to good, anyone could. That's what I always believed.

Black made me question that.

He made me question if it was possible for anyone to <u>want</u> to change, or if God forced people to change. I ain't like to question God, but Black's ways always puzzled me. I could never figure why he just ain't wanna do right. That night when he almost killed me for the last time, helped me to let that go. Black wasn't my problem. He was no longer the wretched soul I'd hope wanna get saved. I prayed for him every now and again, but when I left Camp Hill, I left my love and care for Black right in that two-bedroom shack. I ain't have no 'mo to give Black. That's what I believed.

Years later that belief was challenged in a way ain't never thought possible.

That challenge left me thinkin' that I might actually be a bit crazy, or maybe just too nice.

Chapter Twelve

Stairway to Heaven

Christmas 1970 was the first Christmas without Black and the first Christmas that I actually got to cook what I like and decorate how I like. And boy did I fix the apartment up nice. Ain't seen no decorations like the ones they had out in Orlando, so I just had a ball gettin' stuff togetha. I had a nice table settin'. I had these pretty glasses for the older ones to drink eggnog and a small poinsettia like the ones they always have at church. I said to one of the ushers one time, that I was gonna have me one in my house one day. She laughed 'cause everybody knew I was married to Black, so me sayin' that was like a joke.

Christmas 1970 wasn't a joke.

The tree the kids got me was so nice. The younger ones helped me decorate and we even got a picture wit me holdin' Larry puttin' the angel on the tree.

It was the beginnin' of a new start in my life as well as a Christmas tradition. I'd hear of families talk about traditions in their home, things they do every holiday. I hated that most of my kids ain't have that when they was younger. Nothin' could really make up for what they loss, but I was happy that I was alive and well to be part of the new. The last twenty-five years were a nightmare. There's no sugacoatin' that, but these next twenty-five and more, God willin', would be the best this life have to offer. Leavin' Black fo' the last time help me to see there's nothin' wrong with startin' over, 'specially if what you started wit wasn't really yours in the first place.

That life wit Black wasn't mine, but I dealt with it to prepare me for the blessins' that was 'bout to come. I made it a point to find the positives dealin' wit Black. I learned strength, I acquired a solid belief in the Lord, that I could do all things through Christ

151

who strengthens me.

I would need that strength soon.

Marley and Angela managin' the mail and maintainin' the food stamps while I was gone was a big help. It really was almost as if I'd never left. The kids were able to go right back to school and Elijah showed me how to look through the paper to find work. Being on welfare helped a bit, but I ain't wanna lean on it for the rest of my life, nor did I wanna lean on my kids. It was time I learned how to make my own money. I already knew how to save, that was easy, but workin' out here was somethin' I'd never done, so I was nervous. But, I ain't had no need to be. I'd hear the kids talk 'bout how mean they bosses were and to be honest, anybody who was able to deal wit Black all dem years, shouldn't be 'fraid of no boss. Black was the worst boss anyone could have. That gave me a lil' confidence that workin' wouldn't be as hard as it sound.

Marley and Angela helped me get Larry in a daycare during the day while I worked. First I started cleanin' houses. Honey, these white people houses was fancy. I ain't never seen no furniture like that. They had all kinds of mirrors, large couches, and big TVs. Ain't even know a TV could be that big. All types of liquor, these huge bathrooms. It got me to thinkin' that I could own somethin' like this one day. I learned to be a good listener dealin' with Black, so I'd hear them talkin' 'bout mortgages, real estate and other types of stuff. I'd ask the kids what some of those words meant and they would 'splain it so I'd know. In Camp Hill, we wasn't 'round white folks too much, but in Orlando, I realized they wasn't all that different. The women I cleaned for was housewives just like me. The only thing that separated us was skin color and money. They all had a bunch of kids and ran a household same as me, but they ain't have to do as much work. They had folks like me and a couple of other women who did it.

All they did was give orders.

I ain't mind workin' and cleanin' these houses, but I wasn't for taken orders from nobody. I left all that wit Black. I knew I wanted to have my own and do things my way.

I cleaned houses for about a year or so, then started workin' at daycares. Figured since I had so many kids and watched so many of my grandbabies, why not make it somethin' I do every day.

Felt at home workin' wit kids.

There were so many personalities, smiles and faces. And they all seem to like me. I'd read to 'em and we'd color togetha. I'd help the teachers keep the young ones in order, and they were sure to mine me. Any person might get tired of being 'round kids all day, but not me.

I thought 'bout the days I used to be in Sunday School wit the chil'ren. I enjoyed that. Back then, I couldn't imagine workin' wit chil'ren or even thought to do it on my own. When I worked at the daycare, wasn't no other place I rather be.

It was then I decided to open up my own daycare service.

When I told my own chil'ren 'bout what I wanted to do, they was happy. I'm sure they wondered if I ever had my own goals besides bein' a wife and havin' kids. To be honest, wasn't 'till I finally left Black I started thinkin' 'bout myself for a change. I only had three of my own left to raise and afterward, all my kids would be grown. Black's kids were much older wit they own families and grandkids. I did what I was 'posed to do and now it was time for me.

I learned real quick, that it paid to be nice to

folk. When you nice, people don't mind helpin' you.

Nice became my biggest bargainin' tool.

I cleaned many house over the years and became close to one of the ladies. Her and her husband took a liking to me. Just so happen he had a house for sale. It only took me two years after I moved, and I'd saved enough money to buy a house. Wasn't in the fancy section where 'dem white folks lived, but there was some nice black folk 'round me doin' just as good. Reminded me of the days livin' wit Uncle Willie and Aunt Martha. There was 'nuff kids 'round for my youngest and the school wasn't too far. They was able to take the bus, which made it easier on me in the mornings. They sold the house to me for $10,000. I only had to pay $75.00 a month. Chile, the way these folks spendin' money on houses, that was a steal back in my time.

Buying that house made my life so complete.

My next move was to start preparin' for the daycare. I hadn't made it pass the tenth grade, so I needed more certificates in order to get started. Wasn't a dream delayed, just one I had to wait on a lil longer but the way my life had changed in a matter of years, made the wait fine by me.

In just a short amount of time, I made enough money to get off food stamps and even have health insurance for myself and the younger ones. We ain't never had no insurance. I was always the doctor, nurse, and everything else.

Wasn't sure if things could get better, but they did. Befo' it got pass my expectations, the Lord had one mo' test for me.

Chapter Thirteen

Charcoal

Thirteen years passed since I left Black. I spent my years workin' at daycares, watchin' the kids and helpin' to run the place. This helped me learn how to manage folks. I remained nice, but I learned to be firm. People was able to take direction from me a lot easier knowin' I wasn't talkin' down to 'em or callin' 'em all kinds of names. I lived that life too long, so I know how it made me feel. Folks like to call that empathy. Havin' empathy help me become a leader in many ways. It would be those leadership skills I developed workin' at the daycare that would get me through.

It was a Thursday.

I'd just got home from work, when I walked into the phone ringin' off the hook. I missed the call the first time rushin' to get the phone, so 'bout ten minutes later the phone rang again. It was from the hospital in Camp Hill. The nurse asked me was I married to Charlie Blacksmith, Sr.

My heart dropped.

I'd gone years without hearin' that name and here he was back again. Somehow, that test I knew was comin' was here. God was danglin' a big decision in my face to see how I'd respond. Black had fell ill and was in the hospital experiencin' his last couple months. I hadn't seen Black since I left. The kids would go back and forth to see him and his family from time to time, but I stayed away. I knew what the Lord would want me to do, but I wasn't sure if my heart was in it. I called all the kids over for a family meetin'.

As cruel as their daddy was, most still had a look of concern. Some of 'em said to leave 'em there, but I knew where that was comin' from and it ain't shock me for 'em to say it. Any person, man or woman, would leave 'em there to live out his days in misery. But I remembered my vows, for richer or poorer, in sickness and in health. I know Black ain't meant none of what he said, but I did. It just ain't sit right for me to leave 'em like he was. Parts of me really wanted to see if he was really that sick. I'm sure this couldnt've been a plea to get me back 'cause there was no way I was goin' back to 'em. I took some time off and went up to Camp Hill along with my girls to see 'bout Black.

When I got there, I couldn't believe what I saw.

I ain't even recognize Black, and he barely recognized me.

I'll never forget the day we first met. He was a strong, charismatic, smooth talker, and look like he lift all types of weights. Now, he was this shell of a man. Frail, skinny, look like he ain't ate in days. He was layin' in the hospital bed, dirty, filthy, and smelled somethin' awful.

There was a K-mart across the street from the hospital and we went to get him some underwear, an under shirt and a pair of pajamas. I asked the nurse for a bed pan and I bathed him from head to toe. Once he was dressed and smellin' good, he looked at me and said, "I feel so clean." His voice so soft and weak.

Made me wonder what happen to all those women he dealt wit. All those kids he had outside of the ones he had wit me and his first wife. What happen to all those people he was so quick to run off wit and why the nurse ain't call them?

Lemme tell ya'll somethin...

They'll be alotta folk come in and out ya life.

A lot.

But those people who done stuck by you, made sure you was OK, maybe fix you a meal every now and then, pray for you, call and make sure you doin' well, those the people you do right by. Those folks that only come 'round when you wanna hang out and drank, party all night, play cards or whatever else people do, those folks ain't gon be there when you need 'em most. Those folk shift wit wind, gone as quick as they came.

That's what happen to Black.

Those folks he neglected me and his kids for was nowhere to be found. Not even the women he cheated on me wit, and trust me there was plenty, couldn't find not one of 'em.

Black could barely speak when I walked in his

hospital room. He was seventy-two and weak. Those days, seventy-two still looked pretty good, but Black looked much older. I got a hold of the doctor and he told me there wasn't much they could do for 'em anymore. Him being a vet help with his coverage, but he ain't have long to live. Maybe 'bout two or three-months tops. They'd planned to release 'em to a nursin' home nearby to finish out his last days and asked me if I wanted to take him. I ain't think much 'bout my answer and told them I would bring 'em back to Florida wit me and care for 'em. I know he ain't deserve it, but it just wasn't in me to let 'em die alone. He still was my chil'ren father. They released 'em to me and I took 'em back to the house to pack him up some clothes

I placed Black in the room and I almost got sick lookin' at the house. It was a mess. Anyone could see it hadn't been cleaned, not since I left. The garbage hadn't been takin' out in months, all kinds critters runnin' 'round. Sheets on the bed old and worn. I cleaned up before we left and decided to leave a note for Black's women just in case they stopped by:

If you cared 'bout yo man, you'd least clean up his house. All these years you and all these women been back and forth wit Black but ain't thought well enough to make sure he was doin' right. Black's headin' to Florida where he'll be spendin' his last days so take a good look at this house now, cause this gon be yo last time.

When I went back in the room, Black was curled up in the bed. He looked like a baby layin' there. I couldn't be angry. He was a tormented soul that was witherin' away. All I wanted to do was show him, for once, what love really felt like. I don't think he ever knew what love was. He ain't know how to love, and when someone don't know how to love, there's no way they can give you what you want. That person don't know what it looks like.

A piece of me was happy to show Black love in its greatest form, forgiveness.

When I got back to Orlando, some of the kids were there to help me get him settled in. I had extra rooms in the house, so I was able to give Black my room, while I slept in the guest bed. I just wanted it to be comfortable for 'em. He asked for his boys by his first wife, but only one came. The others didn't want to have anythin' to do wit 'em. I think for some of the kids seein' their father like he was, put things in perspective. Everyone was 'bout to learn a lesson on forgiveness and I was glad to be the teacher.

I became like charcoal.

We all know folks use charcoal for grillin' food, but in the old days, when they had people who specialized in natural healin', charcoal was used to draw poison out the system. If you had a snake bite, or ate some leaves that had those chemicals inside it, crunchin' down on some charcoal and drinkin' a cup of water would bring the poison right up. Cleanse yo system of all the nasty inside.

That's how I was to Black durin' his last days.

I stepped in wit the poison still on his heart, still eatin' away at 'em, even after everybody left 'em for dead and kept him alive just a 'lil while longer to see the poison removed from his body. Most of my kids and only three of his eldest saw him in his last days. They'd talk to 'em a bit, let 'em play with his grandkids. Even his youngest, Myra and Larry saw 'bout they daddy and spent a few minutes wit 'em.

He couldn't keep much down, so I kept broth in the house and fed 'em that wit water. Some days he'd be able to drink tea, but mainly soup and water was all he could muster.

When I brought Black to Florida, it was Spring of 1983. In May 1983, Black took his last breath in my house.

That evenin', there was a pull in me to check on 'em. When I walked into the room, he was up lookin' straight into the ceilin'. I knew then there wasn't much time left. I grabbed the rockin' chair I had in the corner, took his hand and began to recite the 73rd Psalm.

I looked at him, a weak feeble man who looked like a skeleton with skin layin' my bed helpless, gettin' ready to breath his last breath in my bedroom. I wondered what went through his mind. I wondered what did he think of me? Was he proud of me? Did he hate me? I had so many mixed emotions. I held his hand and looked into his eyes and said, I forgive you. He squeezed my hand hard as he could, which was barely a baby's grip, turned to me and mouthed I'm sorry wit tears in his eyes.

I called the kids over.

They gathered in the room to say their goodbyes and moments later, he was gone. A dark chapter in my life had finally closed and I'd given and received the closure I needed.

Life Ain't Been No Crystal Stair

My kids were concerned 'bout me stayin' in this house, but Black's spirit couldn't bother me. I let 'em go and he went. See, once the charcoal removes the poison from yo body, you gotta recover. You gotta get well again and regain your strength. Black got up 'nuff strength to finally apologize to me. It ain't matter whether he did it 'cause he was finna die or not. We all knew how mean and cruel Black was, so really, he ain't have to fix his mouth to say nothin' at all. He coulda just laid there and died. But because I showed 'em mercy, after everythin' he done to me and my kids, even in his last days, he realized that I was the only person, probably on God's green Earth, that truly loved 'em.

That healed his heart, even in death.

That healin' ain't leave no bad spirit or energy in my house. I did get a new bed, 'cause we country folk still a bit superstitious, but I wasn't 'bout to buy a whole new house 'cause Black died there. Honey, that was the end of an era. And sometimes, things need to truly die before they can begin.

I grieved Black's death, then moved right on with my life. For the first time ever, I was truly free.

That's what forgiveness did for me.

That's what bein' a poisonous man's charcoal did for me.

Chapter Fourteen

The Crystal Stair

The kids helped me get Black's affairs in order soon after the funeral. Ain't nobody wanna keep the house, so it just remained there 'till it was torn down. It took time, but in 1986, I opened up my own daycare service.

Ain't take long for business to pick up.

I had so many people lined up to get in, and I hired my granddaughter LaToya to help out in the summer. For the next fifteen years, I watched so many chil'ren come in and out of my daycare. Prolly watched most of the town at some point. I was watchin' the kids of the kids I used to keep.

When I was eighteen, I knew there was more to the life I lived. I knew there was goodness to be had. I just ain't know how to get it or where to start. I ain't really had no one to guide me either. What I learned is that the choices I made or just me wantin' what I ain't have so bad, led me down a path that turned out to make me stronger than I could've ever been. I always wondered what my life would be like had I not married Black. If I'd listen to my Aunt Martha and Uncle Willie when they went 'gainst me datin' 'em, or even left the first time he put his hands on me. To be honest, I ain't sure I woulda turned out how I did. I definitely wouldn't have all of my kids, their kids and beyond.

Can't nobody 'splain why God put us in all these situations, but what I can say is, there's always lessons to be learned. The answers don't always come right away but, eventually, we discover what they are. My lesson was perseverance. I lost everythin' at such a young age to gain more than I could've ever imagined. I wanted a family, I got it. Wasn't the way I saw it in my head, but I got it. Black and I bore twelve chil'ren but all eighteen are mine.

Me.

Life Ain't Been No Crystal Stair

I had twelve babies, and all I ever wanted was a mother and father. I couldn't imagine, then, havin' twelve kids and 'nem havin' kids, and they kids havin' kids. From those twelve and Black's six, I got over sixty grands and great-grands.

Honey, that's family!

I ain't need no mother and father for that. Those kids I raised was me all by myself. The blessins' that are chil'ren is somethin' to shout about, 'cause it's so many people who can't have none and I got sixty.

I wanted to move to a big city and explore what this life had to offer. It took me over twenty years, but I moved to Orlando. Not only did I move to Orlando, I bought a house and started a business wit my own money. All those years livin' with Black, poor for no reason at all, I finally got to a place where myself and my kids ain't have to want for nothin'. I helped other families and mothers just like me, get to a place where they ain't have to want for nothin'. I was able to pay my blessins' forward.

I was timid and shy when I was younger. Ain't have a mind to speak up for myself, and 'cause of that, I endured years of abuse from my husband. Despite that, I ain't let that man break me. I leaned on the strength of the Lord and my kids to get me through. Even helped some of them escape the environment I brought 'em in so they could live a life I couldn't give 'em at the time. There was plenty days I just wanted Black to beat me till I die, but my spirit wouldn't let me. I couldn't leave my kids, even the ones I ain't give birth to. It wasn't a matter of if Black would stop beatin' on me, it was when was I leavin' cause Black was never gonna stop. I had to make him stop.

And I did.

Right around the time Black died, I really got a chance to talk with Lily. She came to the funeral to pay her respects. She ain't shed a tear and I ain't blame her. She was the one I wish I coulda done more for. I understood why she was so resentful towards me. She told me more about her life before I showed up and married her daddy. Her and her siblings ain't never had a chance. It's like their lives were set up to fail from the beginnin'. In my hope to give 'em some peace of mind, I failed in that area. It bothered my spirit so. Reconcilin' wit her allowed both us to say how we really felt. That was more important for her than me. She needed to know, from me, that her feelins' meant somethin'.

Lily meant somethin'.

Life Ain't Been No Crystal Stair

If there was anyone out of our family who persevered the most, it was Lily. When the first man that's 'posed to love you do you wrong, treat you like you don't mean nothin', that does somethin' to a young girl's mind. Her bein' able to stay strong through that, deserved all the respect I had in my body.

Honey, life ain't been no crystal stair for me.

Cinderella lifestyles ain't made for everybody. It's so many of us that scrape the bottom before we climb to the top. I was one of those people. Like I said, my story ain't different from many, but what makes me and other women just like me different, is how we got through. I found the light at the end of the tunnel, walked out that tunnel and never looked back.

I'm grateful to the people that helped me along the way. The Ms. Anns and Mr. Shepards of my life. Those people kept me sane. Women like my Aunt Barb that came and shook things up when life started to get stale. Crazy as it seems, I'm grateful for Black. He was the best teacher I could've ever had. I learned so many life lessons through him and I learned so much about myself. I had to be a grown woman with six kids at eighteen years old. There was no time to hang out with friends, play or do all that stuff young people do now.

I was a mother and wife.

That lifestyle eventually helped me start my own business. Would I have opened up my daycare had I not experienced what I did with Black? I'll never know. However, bein' able to change the ink you write your story with, is the greatest free will the Lord gives us. No matter how hard Black tried to write the story of my life, I was determined to take the pen back and be my own storyteller. I'm not defined by my past. I'm not a widow of an abusive husband, I am Roxie Rae Farrow, business woman, mother of 18 and matriarch of this family.

That is who I am.

That is who I will leave this Earth as.

The pressures of life allowed me to burst into my own diamond and pave the road of my life with those crystals to change my story. Never be 'fraid to change yo story. You never know whose life you'll bless along the way.

Afterword

My grandmother defines survivor.

In her own way, she battled a proverbial cancer. Domestic violence is a cancer and the only cure is yourself. It's one of the biggest lessons I learned from her.

The second was how to fight.

I empowered myself through her story, knowing that if she could survive decades of abuse, have death pass her over, and still become the successful woman she turned out to be, there was no way I could allow something like Colon Cancer to take me out so quick.

So I fought.

I fought just as hard as she did and wouldn't allow this sickness to break my spirit. That's what kept my grandma—her spirit. Her perseverance to see it through. The belief that a light waited for her at the end of the tunnel. That there is always darkness before the dawn but that in the darkness is how we build our strength. We live one day at a time. The same as we put on our pant legs, shoes and shirts. There's no elephant too big to be devoured. No mountain too high to climb. I learned that from my grandmother's story and I hope that same message spoke to you.

About the Author

Born in 1975, Dr. LaToya Hicks grew up not far from one of our most beloved tourist attractions, Disney World in Orlando, Florida. She has always been inspired to write and create having wrote her first play by the second grade. She is a voracious reader who has been heavily influenced by writers ranging from Alice Walker to VC Andrews, Jacquelyn Smith, BeBe Campbell Moore and E. Lynn Harris to name a few. Living in Atlanta for the last two decades LaToya has focused her time on raising her son Marlon Coley Jr and working a full-time career in Finance while continuing to dream and write. She believes whole heartedly in creating the life that you want and thinks one of the best things about being an author is the ability to create and let her imagination run wild. Dr. Hicks completed her Doctorate in Business in 2018.

Acknowledgements

First and Foremost, I would like to thank my maternal grandmother Dennie M. Hicks (Farrow) who was my inspiration and motivation to write this book. It was her courageous life that inspired me to want to create a story that would hopefully shed light on abuse in all forms and encourage women like herself to know that there is life beyond pain and heartache. She is hands down the strongest person that I know. I would like to thank my Mom Betty Jean Hicks Gordon for believing and nurturing my hopes and dreams from a very young age. When God gave out moms I was so lucky and fortunate that you were chosen for me. I want to thank my paternal grandmother Annie J Ramirez for all her love and support and amazing sense of humor that helped to shape who I am today. I want to thank Ken Robinson for being a source of strength and love whenever I needed it throughout my journey. I want to thank all my teachers throughout my life but special thanks to my Kindergarten teacher who happened to be my childhood best friend's mom Mrs. Bobbie McKenzie. She was not only a phenomenal teacher, but It was in her home where creativity was always allowed to flourish. To my 3rd grade Teacher Mrs. Leudenburg who introduced me to the first author who captured my creative heart Judy Blume with Superfudge. Thank you for the incredible gift of story. I want to thank my Dad Ronald Beckett Sr. and all my aunts and uncles on both sides of my family who contributed in various ways to my upbringing. Special shout out to my aunts Margaret Robinson, Anne Newsome and Dera Hicks-Jones who gave me inspiration for my characters in the book through their experiences growing up. My sisters and brothers have always had my heart and I want to thank all of them for their contribution to my life. A special shout out to my baby brother Maurice Hicks who inspires me by staying strong despite life's circumstances. To my nieces and nephews and many cousins thank you for your love and support. To my core friends including my best friend of nearly 30 years Kristina White thank you ladies for your years of inspiration and support and for showing me what true friendship looks and feels like.

Last but certainly not least I want to thank my first love, my son Marlon Markeith Coley Jr. who has been the reason why I have constantly tried to strive for nothing short of excellence in my life. My life changed for the better the day he was born and my love for him runs deeper than anything that I have ever known.

Special dedication to my friend Rolonda Freeman who passed away in 2011. She is the sole reason I moved to Atlanta which is ultimately the place where I developed wings to soar. Her gift of laughter and friendship will forever be missed.

www.ingramcontent.com/pod-product-compliance
Lightning Source LLC
Chambersburg PA
CBHW070933250626
47159CB00009B/3231